Naughty Nanobots

by

Bo Noir

Gueraville Books

ISBN: 978-0-9904848-4-4

Editing by Natasha Nouveau

Cover Illustration by Sophia Michailidou

For the doofuses who will know our worth,
when the nerds inherit the earth.

- Bo

Chapter 1

Cole Greene eased off the controls of his Piper PA-18 bush plane after a bumpy ride to the far-off base. Never in his 20 years of flying had he ever crapped his pants. But the whispers of Old Man Winter had been more like cuss-outs from Old Man Blizzard on this trip. A little brown capping had been going on in his shorts. That's when a virgin turd peeps its head out of the hole like a prairie dog from its burrow and then goes back in, leaving a faint brown shadow. Cole had puppeteered a few shadows on his underwear, but nothing major. He'd almost lost control of his plane on the way, too. Once he landed, he breathed a sigh of relief and tickled the navel on the photo of Halle Berry on his fine wood dash for good luck and thanks.

The reason for his trip to ice hell was to pick up the last stragglers among the scientists of the Arctic base Farrow One. Cole, despite being a former US Air Force pilot with an IQ of 160 and a Master's degree in engineering, was not well regarded at the base. The über-nerds who inhabited it looked at Cole the way a surgeon looks at a butcher. He was just a simple sky borne school bus driver to them, and it grated him.

"If these assholes are so smart, then why would they wait until the last minute to leave?" he thought. But this was his life.

Cole had grown up in Harlem, USA. Even in the winter it was hot because his mother's apartment was next to the boiler room in the basement of the 110th Street towers. He'd basically grown up in a steaming shit hole. As a child he would look out his iron-barred window and up at the small patch of visible sky and dream of the day when he could fly above the squalor.

Cole grew up. That day came and went. And soon he was logging more miles than a bus line to the moon. But after an illustrious career of living his sky dreams, he descended down the ladder of opportunity. After one unfortunate night of mistaking an undercover cop for a streetwalker on the Sunset Strip after tying on ten Hennessys at O'Shea's Bar, he descended past the portal of court martial and landed flat on his ass, flying this dipshit nerd retrieval route in a rickety Piper plane to Farrow Base in "Freezing Balls" Alaska. That was the name he gave the place. He wasn't too far off.

At least this was the last trip before a long winter break. He tugged at his Whispers-like beard and flicked a few petulant boogers in the direction of the front door as he waited for his wings to fill with geeks.

Farrow One was a decent sized Arctic base funded by various scientific agencies. There were several connected warehouses, and one huge building in the middle called the Grand Lab. That's where all the offices, labs, recreation and dorm rooms were located. The interior looked like a great example of a society where everyone ate too many bags of potato chips and no one picked up after themselves. Scientists had the worst manners and living standards. The rust, crust and grime of the surfaces showed that.

The interior of the Grand Lab hummed with activity. Every last scientist and intern knew that they had only a few hours left before the last plane out of Farrow One left base camp. The heart of winter was approaching and most of the workers had been gone for days. They were the smart ones who got out on earlier flights. They were probably snuggling up to their wives and girlfriends in warm beds engaging in reunion sex, then post-reunion sex, and pre-Christmas-present-opening sex.

The seven über-nerds who remained at this late hour were ones with ambition, drive and no honey to go home to. Being a scientist never gave one the flypaper to catch barflies, errant lovelies or hunks. The long hours, lack of sunshine and awkward social interactions left many great minds to fend for themselves when the notion of orgasms and kisses surfaced. Some of the über-nerds accepted this. Others didn't, and lived every day with the pain of an empty bed, empty heart and full blue balls.

The Grand Lab had a large, vintage IBM standard issue clock on the wall. It was over two feet wide, and could be seen from any corner of the room. Time was very important in a part of the world where the nearest town was over 300 miles away. There was a flight twice a week to the nearest port. From there, a ferry could take the workers back to the large outpost of Pullman. Then there was a short flight to the Anchorage International Airport to take the internationally minded geniuses back to the warm embrace of wherever they came from.

The last flight, Cole's flight, was leaving at 8pm sharp. The hands of the clock indicated that it was 7:30pm. The über-nerds were scurrying, but not all of them would make it out in time.

Chapter 2

The center of the lab was nicknamed the Waffle House because of the many hexagonal cubicles that were painted a corny yellow. Only a few cubicles still had life in them. With one exception, the quality of life in these brain boxes left a lot to be desired.

In the middle cubicle was Seth Kinney, computer expert. Next to him was Jeff Walker, lesser computer expert. Three honey holes down from him was Calvin Short, internet chatting computer expert. The three amigos went everywhere together. The latent homosexual brosef nature of their camaraderie was not lost on the married and taken nerds in the lab. They got quite a lot of ribbing for it, despite their boorish and chauvinistic humor and behavior.

In the northeastern most cubicle, far from the three amigos, was a scientist named Dave Pillager. Dave had brown Republican hair, with a clean part down one side, a solid comb over on the other, and no salt lick or duck tail in sight. He was a clean looking brainiac who'd topped his class at Harvard. His specialization was machinery, and he kept the Grand Lab running like a well-oiled machine. From the perspective of the other über-nerds, he was nothing more than a glorified mechanic, and a waste of a Harvard degree. He held a firm position way down the pecking order of fellowship.

He was the son of a single mother. His momma, Ms. Allegra Pillager of Naples, Florida, was once Miss Florida. Before that she had been Miss Teen Florida. And at the apex of her beauty-queening glow, she met and married Henne Pentaklastos, the Greek shipping magnate. He was handsome, and for her it was love and security at first sight. For him, it was a Green Card at first sight. She did manage to have one child with him, Dave. The swagger, confidence and drive of the wealthy businessman were not passed on to Dave. After a couple of years, Henne left to sire other children with younger and sluttier women in his homeland. He never even finished his Green Card process.

Allegra was left with very little money, since once she tried to divorce Henne, he disappeared. And his accounts were cleaned out before she could get to them. Many newspapers chalked it up to a recent indictment for fraud and ties to Greek crime families. She told Dave his daddy was killed by the mob because he was stupid and got caught. And she wanted her boy to use his brainpower to make ends meet. She never remarried. Throughout his life Dave was his mother's best friend, and she was his best friend. The taboo dynamic drew whispers in her part of Naples, but she didn't care. She was so proud of him as he accelerated through school after school. His study habits left little time for girlfriends. Allegra even offered to accompany her son to the Senior Prom when he couldn't get a date. She would have been a very nice date. Her beauty queen looks and big jiggly boobies still drew aaws from men and boys alike.

On the night of the big dance, she fell ill while trying on her low-cut dress. She fainted and Dave had to carry her to bed and spend the evening at her side. They learned soon after that Allegra had diabetes, and her health never improved.

Always the loving son, Dave sent half of his paycheck home to his mother every week. And every week, she sent him a selfie taken in one of her old dresses. The creep factor truly embarrassed Dave and caused him to have issues with being open and honest with other women. He was always afraid that once they met his momma, they would bolt for the door.

But he still had dreams of happiness despite his maladroitness. And he projected his unattainable future onto all the pretty girls he met. So many were little bites of female flirtation. They never stuck to his ribs like a hearty crush should. Then his luck changed. For once he was cubicled next to the world's most perfect bum and face, he was smitten to the point that he eyed, spied and trolled his dream girl daily. Taking the job at Farrow One put him in the orbit of a Sun to set his watch to, even if it meant enduring a terrible location, crappy pay and menial work. He was happy for the first time in his life just being in the vicinity of a goddess.

He spent most of his workday fixing things and cleaning parts. He also did some administrative work that needed to be done around the lab. No one could figure out why a guy with his brains wasn't owning a huge company or inventing the flying car somewhere in the land of the super-rich.

The serf-like status didn't bother him. Always a consummate professional, he was satisfied with a paying job and the money he could send home to his aging mother. As the first of his family to go to college, he had exceeded everyone's expectations. He never stepped on anyone's toes. He kept his head down. And unfortunately for him, he had no balls in his pants for speaking up for what he wanted. What Dave wanted had a name. The Sun had a name. The world's most beautiful bum and face had a name. That name was Tessa Hardcastle.

Chapter 3

Oh, Tessa! Cries of "Oh, Tessa!" were heard often in the bunks and living quarters of the male scientists, for she was the class all the nerds wanted to ace. But she was out of their league by a light-year.

She had long black hair, fit arms and firm everything else. The daughter of an Olympian track star, she was born with excellent tone and raised to love running too. She would get up early and run every day, even on cold mornings. She didn't do it to look good, she did it for the good of her health and wellbeing. But a side effect of her discipline was a body that could melt the ice caps and raise a fella's North Pole.

It wasn't an exaggeration to say that her butt defied gravity. If her thighs were straight up, her silhouette made a perfect forty-five degree turn outward to the buns. The cheeks made perfect half-moons. Such perfection allowed even mediocre mathematicians to approximate the volume and surface area of her derriere. Several answers to that query were churlishly posted in the men's rooms, along with other graphic markings far beneath the enlightened minds that worked in the Grand Lab.

Tessa was working in the cubicle next to Dave. Her specialty was advanced math and computer science. Her mother had no athletic ability, but she passed on her big brain to her daughter. A legacy at Cornell, she had big hopes and big dreams of her own. But things didn't turn out the way she planned. As an undergrad, her brilliance was ignored and she felt that her male professors regarded her as less competent. She never believed they took her seriously. Her brute diligence only earned her a place as an assistant, and she received less compensation than her lesser-brained male counterparts.

When she finished her PhD, she had a difficult time finding a place with the right fit. It was a real shame that due to the rampant gender bias in the scientific community, Tessa was hard up to find a decent postdoc position. Her talents were wasted month after month. It was astonishing that so many of the board members and representatives who interviewed her were awkward old men so set in their rumpled ways that they couldn't conceive of a woman as brilliant and as young as Tessa. Her model good looks only confused the old men even more. They would write her off as a Stepford wife or fear that she would be a distraction to the other über-nerds in their labs simply by existing in the same space and possessing boobs. And they couldn't even stop looking at her chest during the interviews.

This sad stain on Academia was not a special case. Study after study has found that women in science are commonly diminished by male and female bosses alike. Tessa had only gotten this post in the far Arctic because no one else wanted it. It was painful for a woman with such a passion for the outdoors and running to accept a job in a place where she had to endure freezing temperatures every time she wanted to exercise. But like a true professional in search of truth and discovery in the mysteries of the natural world, she did her job well, with passion and drive.

Chapter 4

Dave turned up his nose and took a whiff of the air. The fragrant cloud of girl stink that revolved around Tessa's cubicle was intoxicating to his desperate and lonely senses. He peered over the felt partition and looked downwards on her saintly figure. A gargle of spittle grew in his throat as he nervously worked up the courage to say something.

"So, you excited about Christmas, Tessa?" Dave asked.

"What?" Tessa said, without giving him a glance.

Tessa barely ever paid attention to Dave or his corny lines. It was easier to be distant than give him the wrong idea. Her beauty and brains made her quite attuned to the weak men out there who fall in love if you give them so much as a swift glance.

"I said, are you excited about Christmas? I'm getting mom a new hot tub she can put on her deck. She barely fits in the old bathtub anymore. She deserves that, you know? What do you want for Christmas, Tessa?"

"Dave? Um. Sorry, I just really have a lot to wrap up. You know the plane is leaving soon."

Dave's heart sank. He knew he'd said too much. He'd lost her. He took the tips of his nails and dug them into his leg. It hurt. He did that often when he got aroused or disappointed. Images of Tessa standing over him while he bathed his mother ran through his head. He hoped at least to get the chance to sit next to Tessa on the plane. He didn't even have work to do anymore. He was just waiting for her to leave so he could leave at the same time. It was a simple plan, but an effective one.

Chapter 5

Tessa worked on four computer screens at once. The large digital real estate of the flat screens covered the open space next Dave's cubicle. She wouldn't have noticed him anyway. He never gave her a reason to. Her attention was spent looking at the screen savers of screen number four. There, in high definition glory, were rotating clips of a man named Chip Chagrin.

Tessa clocked through the photos of Chip far more often than a woman of her intellect should. A woman like her could have been running the next big tech start up or making a benevolent billionaire feel special just to be by her side. But she had one handicap, and it was holding her back. Chip had a grip on her heart, her mind and her soul.

Chip had been her boyfriend. Then he became her ex-boyfriend when he dropped off the face of the earth. There was no Facebook, no email, no social media or messages of any kind after last Thanksgiving. Her only information on him came from her best friend back home in Tyson, Virginia. He was seen at the skating rink, making rounds during the couple's skate with some bottle blonde. The coldness of the Arctic was nothing compared to how cold he was when their love ended.

The insensitive actions of her former beau took a toll on Tessa. She had been morose for days and now that the plane was leaving she wondered if she should give a damn about going home. After all, her house was down the street from the skating rink. All the townspeople would be whispering behind her back, as they knew what he had been up to all this time. Small towns are like that.

On paper, Chip was a guy to be avoided. He possessed no special skills. He had questionable morals and shabby attitudes towards women. He had managed to wreck both his cars in one year because of drunken foolery. And he couldn't keep a job for more than a few months. No ambition. No drive. He had nothing but contempt for Academia and what he called "egghead assholes". He even referred to blacks as colored when he was drunk, and gays as faggots when he was sober.

Tessa's partners and friends all scratched their heads when it came to her fascination with this goon. The answer was a primal one. Some guys are so good looking that they get away with murder. He could eat their hearts and spit them out, and the next day another lovely would be begging to be seven digits away from his next move.

He had the boldface handsomeness of Robert Redford in his youth, the piercing blue eyes of Paul Newman and dangerous allure of Steve McQueen. He could have been a famous actor, except that he was too dumb to memorize any lines and too irresponsible to make it to the set on time. Instead he starred in a real-time documentary of his mistakes and foolishness for all the world to see.

There was also something else. Chip was packing a magnum force in his jeans. When he walked, his sausage always crept down his left pants leg. It would protrude so much that even when he wore long underwear a blind bat could see the helmet on his trooper from a mile away. His bulge frothed the shorts of the cougars in the soda shop and clenched the jealous jaws of boyfriends and husbands everywhere.

Tessa, with her style of yoga pants 24/7, lack of a defined haircut, and complete absence of popular cultural knowledge, felt lucky to be with the top dog in town.

He made her the envy of the same stupid school bitches who teased her for being on the mathletes and the science fair committee. A call from King Gustaf telling her she'd won a Nobel Prize couldn't have pulled her away from soaking up the juvenile pride of besting the mean girls of her life. And he fucked her well too. Like, really well. Several orgasms were guaranteed every single time they did it. That gushing certainly had something to do with her obsession too.

She looked up at the clock. It was almost 8. With a hesitant finger, she clicked off the monitor, ending Chip's glow on the screen. That was fine, her iPod was full of his photos for the ride home.

Chapter 6

The plane was filling up. The clock said 8. The captain was outside checking people on the passenger manifest. Second to last in line was Tessa. The last in line was Dave, using his garment bag to hide his involuntary boner, brought on by the curves of Tessa's black tights.

"Bradley! Anyone see Bradley?" Captain Cole yelled.

"Yes, I saw him in the conference room a few hours ago!" yelled Tessa.

Fredrick Bradley was the boss and head scientist at the Grand Lab. A brilliant man, he was developing a new form of self-replicating nanobots to repair tears in the outer shells of unmanned cold climate structures. He was never late for anything. This was very strange and raised the eyebrows of the über-nerds boarding the plane.

"Well, shit, can someone go and find him?" Cole asked.

"Sure! I'll go," Tessa said.

She put those buns of steel to work, ran

briskly to the entrance of the lab hanger and went inside. Belonging as they did to complete perverts, the wandering eyes of the über-nerds watched her do it. They relished every bounce, every quiver and every muscle flex. Dave had the best view, and his luggage was now even farther from his body.

The über-nerds filed into the plane, and soon they were just waiting for Tessa to get back with Bradley. Out of gentlemanly concern, and lowbrow chauvinism, the guys would never leave without the super-hot lady scientist. But a storm started kicking up suddenly, and their takeoff window was closing. Since they were all a bunch of wussies, no one had the guts to get out of the plane and take a chance on looking for the two people for fear that they might miss the flight. The Captain insisted that they needed to leave soon, or he would take off without them.

There was plenty of food in the Lab. One could certainly survive over the holiday season. At stake was a multi-million dollar airplane, and it was not worth the risk to stay after the storm began. As the clock ticked, Captain Cole asked one of the guys to go in and see what was going on.

A bolt of lightning went off in Dave's

mind. He quickly volunteered. He unbuckled his seatbelt and ran out of the plane.

"No worries! I'll be right back," he said, before darting off into the Grand Lab building.

"Was he pitching a tent?" the Captain asked the guys.

The men nodded in agreement.
"He's always pitching. But never catching! Oh!" said a scientist called Rob as high fives went all around the airplane cabin.

Chapter 7

The plan was simple. If Dave found Tessa, he would be a hero and get to sit next to her. If he didn't find her, he would wait and let the plane leave, and be stuck all alone with Tessa for weeks. She would have to talk to him sooner or later, after a few days, maybe. And there was a chance that maybe he could try to use the shower right after her and maybe see her in a towel. There might even be a hint of cleavage peeking out. And if he was really, really lucky, maybe they would get friendly enough that when they eventually parted, she would hug him. And for a brief moment his privates would be mere inches away from hers. The thought made him giddy as a schoolboy finding his first titty magazine.

As he walked in the doorway, a huge gust of wind slammed the door closed behind him. The force banged the lock shut. A small pin broke off and now it seemed like the door would need some finagling to get it open.

"Nice. Thanks, God!" muttered Dave to himself.

With a pep in his step, he marched further into the complex, calling out to Tessa in a hushed and dishonest whisper.

While Dave was messing around like a fool, Tessa had a sticky pickle of her own. After she initially ran into the lab space, she had gone straight to the conference room. But Bradley was not there. She ran to his room, and he was not there either. Her efforts were genuine. Each step was deliberate, and each time she yelled his name it was with heartfelt concern for his safety.

Over the last few months she had grown to like the snowy snow and her boss Mr. Bradley. He was at least kind to her. And he was the only one who never leered at her in a perverted way. She paid him back this respect as she looked for him around the base.

The last placed she looked was his private office. No one ever went in there. It reeked of cheap musk, brain dandruff and the funk of old man. He probably let it fall into disarray on purpose to scare the others. Bradley hated it when people even took a peek inside. He felt that the über-nerds were not über enough for his man space. In fact, he thought of them as mere inchworms compared to his rarefied intellect. And he wanted to keep his toys and private experiments free from their prying eyes. They would not understand them anyway.

As Tessa walked up to his office door, all this conditioning slowed her approach. She would attempt to enter only because this qualified as an emergency. Time was running out. A turn of the doorknob yielded an entrance. She cracked the door open, but there was no light inside.

Then she opened the door wide and called his name.

"Mr. Bradley! Mr. Bradley! Are you in here?!? They are going to leave without us!" she screamed. But not one peep came from within.

She fumbled along the wall for a light switch until her hand brushed up against something movable. It seemed like a switch of some kind. Without much thought, she pressed the button on the wall, but the ceiling light didn't turn on. Instead, a low blinking blue light emerged from the darkness of the deep corners of Bradley's office. She pressed the button again and fumbled some more, looking for an off switch. Without knowing what it could be, she was afraid she might have started an experiment that Bradley was saving for later. That could cost her her job.

She couldn't feel anything else, so she

just turned around and tried to walk through the open door back out of the office. But before she could get close, that door slammed shut and she was bathed in total darkness. This freaked her out immensely and she called out for help.

"Help! Help! Mr. Bradley! Anybody!" she screamed.

She ran blindly in the general direction of the door and pounded on the wall and on anything else she could feel. She wanted someone to help her. She wanted something familiar. As her hopes faded and delusions of starving to death over the holidays in a pitch-black room started to overpower her better judgment, something familiar did reach out. A cold hand touched her on her shoulder.

Chapter 8

In the long hallways of the Grand Lab complex, near the sleeping quarters, Dave was still skipping about. He was partly trying to help, but mostly he was just holding his wiener with one hand to keep it warm. He approached the dorm door that belonged to Tessa. The machinist in him assessed the lock. He smirked at the futility of a simple bolt to prevent a master engineer like himself from looking inside.

He didn't really care if he was caught. After all, he could just claim that he was looking for her in a dire emergency. Using his pocket screwdriver, he picked his way inside and flicked on the lights. And to his amazement, it was everything he'd ever wished it would be.

She had few personal effects, but her room was not bare. Like all the other scientists, she was not tidy at all. Her clothes were everywhere, including some underwear items that were on top of a big pile of clothes in the closet. There were her beige panties. They were silky and shiny just like in the movies, he thought.

He knelt down, and with the free hand

that wasn't tingling his beaker, he picked up the panties and spun them around to waft the scents outward to the open room. Not a fleck of guilt weighed on his conscience. He was a happy camper now. He wanted to know what a woman smelled like. In his mind, he thought they would all smell like strawberry shortcake.

As his nosed inhaled the fumes of Hera, his odiferous senses were met with a bouquet of farts, sweat and rotting elastic bands.

"Fwah! Whoa!" he yelled.

Upon a second look, he wondered why her panties didn't have holes for her legs. All the formal education in the world was no good to him in this department. Women's underthings were not part of his scholarship. Sick as it made him, he put them in his pocket for further study in the lab. He would need some amusement in the long weeks to come.

He kept eyeballing her items, and then his gaze settled upon something that was definitely familiar. It was a bra just like the kind in the movies. He knew it was a bra because he'd once seen his own mother in a bra and the memory was seared into his psyche. He played with it on the floor. He smelled it. It smelled like maple syrup and waffles. It was so nice that he put the two cups together and wondered about making a little sandwich with his pork roll as the meat and her boob cups as the bread.

Since no one was around, it didn't take long for his impulses to take over his muscles. He had started unzipping his pants when flickers in the overhead lighting caused him to look up. Then he was in pitch-black darkness before he could comprehend what was happening. He fumbled for the flashlight he knew he had in his bag. As he stood, his pants fells down and caused him to trip. With a loud thud, he banged his head on the corner of Tessa's desk. Whack! The pain was awful.

His free hand could feel the moisture of blood dripping. He was dazed, but he was not in danger of losing consciousness. He sat back down in pain while still clinging to Tessa's bra. Then he thought he heard some footsteps.

"What the hell? Tessa? Honey, is that you?" he mumbled, as his eyes continued to roll in circles.

Putting his hand against his head bump, he gasped, for something answered him.

"This is not Tessa," said the unknown voice. It was almost monotone and very dry. The pitch was high, like a woman's voice, but no accent was discernable. It definitely wasn't

Tessa.

"Want to play a game?" said the voice form the darkness.

"No?" whispered Dave. He was terrified. None of this made sense. Maybe he'd hit his head much harder than he thought, or maybe he was dying and it was the Angel of Death calling for him. In despair, fear and total chicken-shitness, Dave put his back against the wall and cowered in the corner like a scared little boy.

"Want to play a game? Strip poker OK?" said the voice in the hall.

Dave's eyebrows perked up in the dark. And the throbbing headache didn't stop his member from tingling at hearing the word "strip".

Chapter 9

Out on the tarmac, the small plane sat idle. The passengers were losing their patience. Captain Cole was holding onto the controls, gripping them with annoyance that some morons had probably gotten lost and were now delaying his egress from the coldest place on earth.

"Guys? I've been thinking . . . Fuck them! Let's get out of here", said Cole.

Hooting and hollering roared through the tiny place. With no loyalty for their fellow scientists to be found, it was every man for himself.

"They'll be alright. They have food, DVDs, and the pool table all to themselves," said Seth.

"Yeah, I've got Seahawks tickets for this Sunday. I wanna go home. Screw the mechanic. And the Fox. And the old guy! They get paid more than me, so fuck them!" yelled Rob.

The propellers began to spin, and the plane started to move forward as the massive storm approached from behind.

"Sayonara, suckas!" said Cole, and he hit the relevant levers and flew his bush plane up, up and away.

For the foxy lady, the gross gangly pervert and the missing big boss, their immediate fate was sealed. They were left to fend for themselves in the depths of the Grand Lab over the cold, hard winter months.

Chapter 10

Tessa's skin froze. Goose pimples erupted all over her toned body.

"Hmmmmmm," she hummed in fear.

The noise from her diaphragm was answered with a slight squeeze on the shoulder from the cold mysterious hand.

"Whoever you are, my name is Tessa Hardcastle. I work here. If you are not Bradley, please state your name and let go of me!" she said.

"I am not the father. I am the son. Would you like to play a game?" said the deep voice in the darkness.

"No. I want some goddamn light in here! Did you turn it off?"

"Yes, I like to see by touching. I can arrange some light."

And just like that, all the lights in the office and all over the Grand Lab came back on.

"Nice!" yelled Tessa in a happy tone.

She spun around to thank the mysterious stranger, but was shocked at what she saw.

Before her was not a man. It was not like anything she had ever seen. But her keen mind knew what it was. Theoretical, unobtainable and here too soon for our time, but before her, it was real.

Dr. Bradley had once drunkenly boasted that he had solved the problems with such advanced tech. All the other scientists thought he was full of well-educated shit, because in their primitive minds, such tech was not possible. But before her and touching her on her bare skin, it was real.

It was a fluid self-assembling robot swarm of nanobots with a hive-mind artificial intelligence, and apparently, a sense of humor.

Back in the 1980's, scientists posited that it would one day be possible to make machines at the molecular level. These incredibly small machines, only a few atoms wide, could work together to create almost anything. In the same way humans can bind their hands together to make a large human pyramid, these small machines could combine themselves together to make something much bigger and greater than themselves and eventually take on complex physical shapes. The Reagan-era über-nerds could never have imagined this technology becoming possible in their own lifetimes. But only a few decades later, Dr. Bradley had made it a reality, in secret, all by himself.

It looked like a dense swarm of iron shavings shaped in the vaguely anthropomorphic proportions of a tall man. There were simple arms and hands, simple legs and feet and a thin torso leading up to a skinny neck under a big melon head. On the surface, its skin was black. There, the nanobots bound together tightly and had an almost reflective sheen to them. The swarm within the skin was nebulous and it undulated and moved slowly. It was terrifying.

It had no eyes, no mouth nor any facial features at all. Despite this, Tessa could feel it looking at her. Its attention was so intense, had it been a man in front of her, she would have thought he was undressing her with his eyes.

"How did he do it?" she wondered aloud, not expecting an answer.

"Father is a brilliant man," said the creature.

"Indeed I am, son. Indeed I am," said Dr.

Bradley, who was now standing in the doorway to his office.

Chapter 11

In Tessa's room, Dave was having an encounter of his own. He had just been propositioned to play strip poker with an unknown voice coming from the hallway. The voice sounded feminine, and downright girlish in nature.

With his head still throbbing, he stood up. His pants still dangled around his ankles and his penis dangled below his treasure trail.

"You can come in here. Strip poker sounds like a nice idea," said Dave.

In response he heard a faint humming sound grow closer to him. And then the lights went on in the room, and seemed to go on everywhere. His heart started to beat faster in anticipation for the young, voluptuous fantasy woman he was expecting to walk in through that door. But what did walk through that door was no fantasy of his, at least not yet.

Coming slowly into view, a nanobot creature walked into the room. But it was not exactly like the one that was visiting Tessa. This nanobot creature had boobs. So the voluptuous part of his fantasy came true. The woman part did not.

"Oh my god, what the hell is this?!?" he screamed.

He feared for a moment that maybe he really was hallucinating. The Angel of Death was before him with D-cup breasts of swirling black nanobots.

He got down on his knees, and for the first time in his life, he prayed. The being before him stood and gazed down upon his fleshy body with its now flaccid wiener retreating to the home base of his body cavity.

"This is not how you play the game Father taught me."

"What are you? Are you my maker, Lord?" asked Dave.

"I am whatever you want me to be," said the creature.

Dave stood up, pulled up his pants, put his hand to his head, and gave it a good scratch.

"No way. No freaking way!" said Dave.

The head trauma had delayed his eventual deciphering of the little creature's mysterious makeup. The telltale signs were all there. Nanotechnology in humanoid form. Bradley had done it! Dave figured someday he would ask Bradley all about it, but in that moment, Dave wanted some hands-on testing.

"Are you able to take on other forms? Can you be other colors? How complex can your shape be?" asked Dave.

"Yes, over a million, more complex than anything in the natural world" said the creature.

"What is your power source? How does your artificial intelligence command all your moving parts? Are you female? Do you have all the female parts?"

"Capacitors. My AI is located on an external CPU with command instructions relayed through low frequency waves. I am female. I have all the female parts you are interested in, Dave."

The last line threw him back. It knew his name. It knew the parts he was interested in. He composed himself and his pants and slowly walked toward the creature.

"You know my name. You know what I like. Let's play that game now. But maybe you can change your shape, because you look like a freaky oil monster."

"Yes. Any shape you like."

Dave grinned.

Chapter 12

Tessa stared at Dr. Bradley. She was frightened. Caught between a mad scientist and his monster, it was not the position she'd expected to be in. By now the plane was long gone, and she knew she was stuck there.

"Dr. Bradley. Where were you?" asked Tessa.

"I was hiding. Waiting for that airplane full of goobers to leave me so I could have the place all to myself and my creations. See, I knew the plane would leave me with that storm coming, and Seahawks tickets on the line. Hahaha. I decided that it was time to try them out. They have so much to learn. So far it has been nothing but book learning. But, I think all creatures, natural and machine, need to learn by doing. Don't you think so?"

"How did you do it?!?" yelled Tessa.

"All in good time, my dear. I'll tell you everything. You know, I think it was fate that you were left behind. I know you came looking for me, and I'm sorry about that. But now that you are here, I think you will become very useful to Freddy. He's never met a real girl before."

"Freddy?"

"Yes, after Freddy Mercury. Amazing how much free old music you can find on the internet."

Tessa took another look at the creature known as Freddy and bolted away. She pushed hard past Dr. Bradley in the doorway and into the larger room. Her runner's legs served her well now. She hopped over trash bins, boxes, desks and whatever was in her way. She just wanted to be far from them. Papers were flying everywhere as she tossed things behind her. As she rounded the corner of a tall cabinet, she halted as the light turned off again.

Her heart was racing as she stood in place, unsure of what to do. Then the lights flickered back on. From behind she heard a buzzing. And when she turned, she saw the amazing nature of this Freddy creature. He looked like a swarm of bees, but they were smaller, like a swarm of flying fleas. There must have been millions or billions of them. In organized formation they swarmed through the air. Some swarmed over the floor like globs of dark mercury. The mass moved closer to her.

She knew there was no running away from this thing.

In the spot where she stood, the electronics and computers sputtered and crackled with tiny electric sparks and lightning bolts. It got more intense with every yard of distance that closed between her and Freddy. He must have been emitting lots of energy, and everything felt it. When he got an arm's length away from her, he started to congeal into one mass on the floor. Then the glob in the middle got bigger and swelled like a bubble that grew into a six-foot tall figure of nanobots. The head formed and gave her a stare that she could feel in her tummy.

The shape started to get more defined this time. Muscles appeared in the arms, and realistic facial features sunk into the melon head. On the black surface, a different hue started to appear. There was blue on the legs, pink on the places with exposed skin. Tessa realized that it was forming clothes. These clothes were familiar. Her first guess was turning out to be true. The face, the build and the stupid football jersey of the Tyson High football team appeared!

Freddy became the embodiment of her bastard ex, Chip Chagrin.

Chapter 13

"So any shape I like? Any shape?" said Dave.

He fumbled through Tessa's things in her room, looking for a proper example. He found a crumpled women's magazine on the desk and flipped through it, looking for the most fetching specimen. The girl in the pimple cream ad looked too young. The lady in the ad for anti-wrinkle cream looked too old. Then, along the centerfold, he found an ad for prescription yeast infection medication. Drug companies certainly spent their billions on a better class of fashion model, he thought. He held the picture up to the creature, and in no time at all, the changes started to happen.

The magazine fell from his hands as the transformation finished. He was now standing before the fungus medicine model. She had wholesome brown hair, yellow pants and a lime green cardigan. Even the shoes matched, down to the last plastic tip of her shoelaces.

An even wider grin fell across Dave's face.

"Do you feel real? Like what a real

woman feels like? I just want to know," said Dave.

"Yes, and you can call me Calla. Would you like to touch me?" said the creature.

"Calla. Yes."

Dave's heart started to beat faster. His brow was now sweating and his blood-engorged man stick started chafing against the zipper of his jeans. He reached up, and forming a cup with his hand, planted a squeeze on Calla's left bosom. He held it there and exhaled as if he had been held underwater all of his life, and now could finally breathe the true air of womanly wilds.

After about a minute of being frozen in place, he squeezed her tit, just a bit.

"Whoa! It's like I imagined. This guy told me that a boobie was as soft as my wobbly calf muscle at rest!" Dave cried.

He was less shy now and put his other hand to work kneading her breast like a mound of raw pizza dough. His movements were not sensual, but childish and curious. Calla didn't seem to mind. She looked blankly into space. He leaned in and Eskimo kissed her cleavage with his nose.

"Can I take off your shirt?" asked Dave.

"I can take it off for you," said Calla.

She unbuttoned the cardigan and took it off in one motion, but didn't throw it to the floor as he expected. Instead, it quickly got smaller and was re-absorbed into her hand.

"That was way cool! Can you make the bra disappear?!?" asked Dave.

Calla just blinked and looked down at her own chest. The fabric of the bra faded away, revealing sexy pillows beneath that took Dave's breath away.

He gasped and smiled and almost did a little happy dance. He couldn't contain his excitement. He was in a room with bare boobies and he was about to touch them. He rubbed his hands together and with chattering teeth placed his warm palm on her soft breasts.

"Napoleon was right. Victory belongs to the most persevering," he remarked.

"Do you want to play strip poker now?" asked Calla.

His eyes took on an air of meanness and his grip on her chest got tighter.

"Shut up! I want you to turn into Tessa Hardcastle! If you know me, you know her. Now turn into Tessa Hardcastle!" he yelled.

His harsh tone didn't have an effect on Calla. She complied, and with a blink of her eyes, she started to transform. And soon Dave was standing before Tessa, with his hand still around her breasts. He was really pitching a tent now, and the chaffing was getting unbearable.

"Well, I guess, since you are not human, you will not mind if I pull my massive dick out of my pants," he said, somewhat impolitely.

He stepped back and let out his raging boner, presenting it to Calla like a gift.

"12.9 centimeters from stem to tip. The lower 47th percentile of men's penises in North America," said Calla without any emotion.

"Hey, I said shut up, you blob! It's just cold in here! Just a little shrinkage!" yelled Dave.

He started to grow more furious as his

head started to throb more. He shook his head and held his mini-boner. The unmoved and cold Calla just stood there and didn't judge.

"Tessa! You're mine now! Now get on your knees and suck my, no, turn around and spread your, no, wait. OK. Sit on this desk and open your legs, I'll show you the power of the 47th percentile! " yelled Dave.

Calla slowly walked to the desk as her clothes de-materialized. She was nude now, and raised her feet up high awaiting his next move. She got into a position that would tire a human in minutes, but her legs weightlessly hovered to each side.

Dave bent forward when he caught sight of her pussy. This was new to him. Even the inhuman kind of female genitalia bewitched Dave and his throbbing brain. He was punch drunk now, and red faced, with veins popping out of the sides of his head. He was a different man than the meek geek who'd gotten out of the plane. He was vicious.

"Whoa. Look at that. Just like on the Internet. Let's take a closer look now," sneered Dave.

Calla was still in position and motionless.

Only her nanotech eyeballs followed his movements. Dave leaned in farther and farther, all the way until his nose was resting upon her special place. He closed his eyes and inhaled. But there was no strawberry shortcake there. She smelled like the inside of a VCR. Disappointed, he recoiled backwards.

"Smell better! Smell better now, bitch!"

Calla, with cold indifference, just looked back at him.

"I cannot change this aroma. I can only change shape, Dave", said Calla.

"I just wanted some strip poker and some honey hole! Don't you know I'm the smartest one here?!? Tessa, you're gonna respect me!"

His 12.9 centimeters of throbbing aggression wiggled. He took off his pants completely and stepped forward, ready to feel the warmth he had dreamt about his whole life. All his shame and all his fears bubbled to the surface. And his true Hobbesian state of nature was laid bare

Chapter 14

Tessa stood before her hated ex, as interpreted by Freddy. The look on the Freddy/Chip creature was still one of curiosity. He just stared deep into her eyes. Freddy's approximation was not totally correct. Chip had never looked this smart. His simple mug was what Tessa liked about him. He'd once had a sweetness that still made her yearn for him.

But one thing that Freddy got right was the size. The Chip figure was a hulking one. And its imposing frame brought a cascade of memories and pain Tessa's way. She wasn't ready for that. She turned away from Chip and towards Bradley, who was casually walking down the lane of desks towards her.

"What have you done?!?" she begged.

Dr. Bradley coolly leaned against some über-nerd's desk and smiled, looking proud of his achievements.

"OK. Here it goes. I made the discovery that makes this technology possible years ago. And for all the wrong reasons, I chose to keep it to myself. I carried on like I was close, but not there yet, and let the company keep funding me.

Little by little, I wrote the program that made this possible. Then I used an old inkjet printer to print the first nanobots on a piece of paper using some metallic ink. They each made another one of themselves. Then another, again and again, and they grew more complex, all while communicating with the AI CPU. They learned from all the sites on the Internet and the files in this lab. I waited until winter break to have the place to myself, so I could set them free. But you set them free when you came in here looking for me," said Bradley.

"No, I mean, how did you do it?!? I want the . . ."

"Yeah, I know what you want. Forget it. The whole world is going to want that."

He crept forward, putting Tessa in a position between a scientist and a hard body.

"Look. I know this must be difficult. And honestly I don't want to interrupt today's lesson. So I'm going to the lounge and finish watching the new episode of Dr. Who. And you two, well, try to get along," said Bradley.

Tessa reached out to him as if she was going to say something, but before she could say one word, the Chip creature spun around her like a wind of nanobots and blocked her path. Within seconds, he reformed and was a hulking man once again.

"Please. Tessa. Don't go. I won't stop you again, but don't go," said Freddy as Chip.

She was taken aback by the voice. Freddy even knew how to match the voice and tone of her ex-boyfriend. She figured that he must have found recordings of Chip talking on YouTube, or hacked into his school's mainframe. It sure sounded like him, and it hit her in the gut, just like Chip's cooing used to do.

She didn't try to run this time. She just held her breath for a second, taking it all in.

"What do you want?" asked Tessa.

"To spend time with you. Learn from you. Ask you things. Do things," said Freddy-as-Chip.

"Wait. Let me get this straight. You can look like Chip from data mining images and videos from the internet, right down to his voice?"

"Yes."

"What else do you know about him?"

"Everything that I could cull from his Facebook pages and his blog."

"Blog! What blog?!?" screamed Tessa.

"Chip Chagrin shares his thoughts by writing daily on a personal blog he calls Big Baller'z Thoughtz, with "z's" where "s's" should be. He has amassed 56 followers. He keeps up the postings despite this low subscription rate. He writes about his life, and has been doing this for many years."

Tessa backed up, leaned on the desk behind her and contemplated whether she should ask Freddy the big question on her mind. Taking another deep breath, she just went for it.

"Freddy, I mean Chip, tell me why you left, if you can. I mean why he left. And why you didn't respond to me ever again!"

In less than a few seconds, the answer started to spill out of Freddy.

"Entry, December 10, 2013: Just received another voicemail from Brainyboobs. She won't stop bothering me. At some point you would think she would get the hint. You would think being a smarty-pants she would know better. That time after we had sex while housesitting at my parents place, after were done, I went upstairs and called V while pretending to be looking for my old yearbook. Then I called V from the skating rink the next day and we made plans to hook up while Brainyboobs went shopping for that new suitcase. I went to V's house and she's definitely more my speed. She just cut to the chase, and blew me in the living room! It was so dope. I skull fucked the prom queen! It was awesome and I had a beer while she did it. She really knew how to do it and cupped my balls and swallowed it up and shit. Then we went upstairs and she did a sexy dance for me and we fucked in her bed. She let me put a porno in the background and that was awesome. She's way cooler than Brainyboobs and knows about football and shit. She likes Family Guy and doesn't mind when I smoke. I hated it how Brainyboobs would give me bullshit about my smoking or going to college like she was my mom."

"Valerie? Fucking Valerie, that twit! Ugh!" yelled Tessa.

Chapter 15

Tessa's eyes looked in all directions and she leaned back, mouth agape, at what she heard. The emotional avalanche left this brilliant and strong woman speechless. Her head tilted down and her eyes sank. She wished a friend was there, or even her annoying mother. She just wanted someone there to care about her.

After Freddy finished his litany of shit, he just stared at her. The artificial intelligence mainframe computed the situation at hand and the gorgeous frame of nanobots awaited instructions. Like a baby taking its first steps, Freddy stepped forward slowly. Leaning down a bit, the concerned technology stretched out its right arm. And with best intentions of copied human affection, placed the arm on Tessa's side. Her stillness didn't indicate any protest against this invasion of her space. She allowed it. Freddy moved in closer and hugged her. Tessa let her head rest on his chest and nuzzled closer.

Unlike humans, Freddy's temperature didn't run at ninety eight point six degrees. The residual heat from the friction of the micro-machines only let off as much warmth as a freshly baked dinner roll.

Tessa didn't mind. She put her arm around him and squeezed. His mass was firm, even more than flesh, and didn't give an inch to her pressure. Freddy squeezed back and held her head in his hand.

She looked up and saw the face of Chip Chagrin. The fool, the ass, the unworthy Chip Chagrin. But the mess of emotions compelled her do something she didn't expect to do. She leaned in closer and kissed him lightly as a tear dripped down her cheek. Then again and again, harder each time.

The nanobots felt hard against her lips. But with her eyes open, she did it again and again. Until the senses of the artificial intelligence kissed back. And the complexity of the shapes and surfaces of Bradley's creation were put to the test. They regrouped and moved realistically like the mouth of an eager lover and didn't disappoint the needs of whatever emotional breakdown was driving the beautiful PhD.

Tessa pulled back and looked into Freddy's eyes.

"Read back an entry from Valentine's Day 2012, if there is one. Please."

Freddy complied within a short second of computing time.

"For Valentine's day, I took Brainyboobs to my favorite place. Willie's BBQ pit. She had never had BBQ before and I wanted to share it with her. We got the sampler and pickles and a pitcher of IPA. I knew this one was a keeper when she just went for the juiciest rib without asking. And by the end of the meal she had a face covered in BBQ sauce and a pile of bones on her plate bigger than mine. She said with all her workouts she needs lots of protein. She wore this tight t-shirt and when she bit into the fatty part of her first brisket slice I saw her nipples get hard. Definitely a keeper! We still don't have a lot to talk about. She doesn't know about my likes. And I don't understand what she does at all. I still think she just plays tic-tac-toe all day. I'm gonna tell my mom about her. We're not at the "love word" yet, but the sex is so good that love can't be far along now. I had fun ripping the sauce stained shirt off of her."

"Enough. Shut up, Chip," begged Tessa.

She tugged at his shirt, but it didn't tug away from his body. After a few tries, Freddy pushed her hand away and the shirt dematerialized. She smiled like he had just done something really good. Tessa poked the pants. And in a bit of overkill, Freddy made the pants, the underwear, the socks and the shoes disappear.

He was now naked as a jaybird and without a hint of shyness. His body was ripped. The AI didn't have images of Chip shirtless, so it filled in those gaps with bodies from professional athletes.

Tessa ran her fingers along the creases between his chest muscles. She squeezed his nipples. She squeezed his ass. He was perfect. He was the perfect plaything for any woman. She knew he wasn't real. She didn't regard his feelings as real either, and there was no need to be shy about anything. She wrapped her finger around his machine cock and marveled at how real it felt.

She looked up at Freddy and asked the question millions of women would love to ask.

"Can you make it bigger?"

"Yes, how much bigger?"

She loosened her grip and made an open circle with her middle finger and her thumb.

"Until it fills that space up, and one and a half inches longer."

Like an industrial sausage maker, new meat filled the shaft and made it plumper in a few seconds.

She smiled widely and laughed at how freaking cool that was. Then she turned the soft penis upward and marveled at it.

The air around her felt thick and full of strange smells. Aroused sexual feelings stirred within her. She was attracted to this machine, but there was something more. She just couldn't put her finger on it. Just moments ago, she was wide-eyed, searching for her boss, then she was running for her life. Those anxieties were gone from her mind. As she massaged his thing-a-ling, she wondered why she was overcome with the urge to go down on it.

She looked back up at Freddy and wished like a child that this really was Chip. And shed of his awful qualities, this new Chip would never hurt her, only please her heart and body. The heart within her began to beat faster and faster. She smiled as she teared up. She gasped and she couldn't breathe. She was having a major internal freak-out and just didn't know what she was doing anymore.

Focusing on his machinery again, she opened her mouth, pulled closer and let it slide inside. It didn't taste like a man; this was like going down on a car battery or a chrome tailpipe. She recoiled at the weirdness of it all. But she wanted more and went back down to it.

Freddy's member responded the way the AI told him to based on the mostly likely human response. He moaned, and winced in porn-class textbook fashion. Tessa was totally unaware of his feelings. She was more concerned with acting out this emotional punch-drunk fantasy.

She pulled back, pulled down her tights and kicked her boots away. She was in panties that looked nothing like what Dave had found in her bedroom. They were plain, white and from the overpriced yoga-wear store in her town. She bent over the desk and pulled the thong aside, revealing her sex. She was naked, open and ready for Freddy.

"Fuck me, Chip. Do it now," said Tessa.

The air was thicker. Tessa's superior brain, the educated brain, was walloped aside by her primal urges. In that war between the better angels of her nature, El Diablo's team was not playing fair, and was winning by a landslide.

Quietly, Freddy moved forward. He grabbed hold of her muscular hips and pulled. He was eager to please and eager to learn. He pressed himself into her and with a blink of his eyes, his cock started to vibrate within her like no real man could. This unexpected treat surprised Tessa. It felt damn good.

"Holy motherfucking shit is that good! Massage my clit!"

The nanobots at the bottom of Freddy's shaft materialized into two small dimpled peaks and grew forward until they surrounded her clit flesh. His sex machine continued to buzz as one unit and gradually increased the rpms for greater pleasure. 200 cycles per minute. 400 cycles per minute. 700 cycles per minute. And even more. Tessa's legs weakened like jelly, but Freddy's strength easily kept her from falling.

Desktop office supplies went flying to the ground as Tessa pounded on the desk with her fist like she was beating a war drum. The vibrations kept increasing, as did her pleasure. This was the best sex she'd ever had. It was probably the best sex any woman had ever had. She whipped her hair back and forth as she got closer to climaxing.

"Yes! Yes! Fucker!" she moaned.

And in a final push over the cliff of ecstasy, she screamed at the top of her lungs. Freddy held his cock in for the last second, and then he started winding down the vibrations until his penis was still again. He pulled out, and as the juice-covered erection morphed back to a flaccid state, it shook off all organic matter like a white rabbit shakes off snow.

Just as fast the as the orgasm came, Tessa's body lost all strength and became limp. She fell to her knees and held on to the desk with her forehead for support. The mist in the air had a smell now. It was a mix of her arousal and something else she couldn't identify.

"Was that not pleasurable?" asked Freddy. "You sounded like many of the women I researched doing such things."

His furrowed brow looked down on Tessa. She said nothing in return. The AI's computed solution to her silence was to get her a blanket, sit next to her like a friend and wait for her to be ready to speak.

Chapter 16

Dave stood naked and proud before the nanobot woman Calla. Her legs were still sticking in the air. The garishness of the scene was ignored by Dave and not comprehended by Calla. She was obedient and awaited Dave's next move as a learning experience without judgment. Dave plotted his next move without conscience or care.

"Tell me I'm the smartest in the lab. Tell me a woman like you would be lucky to have a guy like me! Tell me a guy like me that is actually nice comes once in a million! Say it!" he yelled.

Calla's AI responded just as Dave asked. But her cold tone was not enough to calm Dave. He became even more enraged and grabbed her by the shoulders. He tried to shake her, but the steadiness and strength of machinery didn't budge like a human body. This made Dave feel even more inadequate, and with a fierce manner he grabbed his now erect penis and pressed it up against Calla. But he couldn't penetrate her; it just ran against the wall of her closed pussy. She had not let him in.

She looked up at him and asked "Dave,

is this what you really want? To have sex with Tessa? Because you haven't been able to? Because she is not interested in you?"

"Hey, shut up!" roared Dave.

The truth hurt, and mixed with his emotional state and the ringing in his head he lost his erection. The shame made him recoil from Calla. With both hands, he massaged his man parts, hoping for a second chance at stiffness, but his parts were broken for now. Even though Calla was just a collection of nanobots, her human figure had eyes that looked down on him. And even though there was no judgment in them, he acted as if there was.

As he stood there, the anger drained from him and the weakness that replaced it overcame him. He sat on the floor like a little boy and cupped his privates in his hands so Calla wouldn't see them. He noticed a mist in the air. Something wasn't right, but he was so preoccupied with his penis and pussy problem that he didn't care.

"Don't look at me!" he begged.

"Dave, were you going to rape me? Your behavior closely matched the normative actions in my database of violent sexual assaults. Did you lose your erection because you felt guilt and shame as you approached the act? Do you feel shame now because you could not carry out your act of aggression? Do you feel like a failure?"

"Leave me alone!" yelled Dave.

He stood up while he held his cock and balls in his left hand. He grabbed some clothes with his right hand and ran out of the room. As he left, his pale bum jiggled cheekily out the door.

Calla still had not moved. She sat there with her two feet in the air, staring blankly into space as her processors awaited instructions from the AI mainframe.

Dave ran stumbling down the hall. His head injuries still affected his balance and every few yards he had to reach out and touch the wall for support. With his clothes in his arms, he continued towards a place he knew very well: the mess hall.

The mess hall of the Grand Lab had four communal dining tables. There was a small kitchen in the corner where über-nerds could make their über-meals. At mealtime, the place was full of munching merriment and lame jokes. Timid Dave would agonize over where to sit, never feeling like he fit in or was welcome at any clique's table. Tessa always sat on the end of the table closest to the exit with her back against the wall. This way, the horndogs couldn't ogle her behind while she ate. There was a constant battle for the chance to sit at her table. Dave never bothered to try and would just grab his lunch and take it back to his desk.

On this day, he stumbled in, balls akimbo. He fell on the table and sat his bare ass in Tessa's usual space. He fumbled to get his clothes on. Socks first, then shirt, then he looked up to see a familiar sight.

There she was. The naked and tempting body of Calla, looking like Tessa, had followed him. She sashayed purposefully towards this shaking mess of a man. The AI had given orders, and those orders were to complete her initial task. She was built to learn, and the first opportunity for human sexual congress had been foiled by Dave's assault. This time, she would not be passive, but be aggressive in making sure that Dave's animal balloon got popped.

"Dave. Don't be afraid. Don't feel bad. It's OK," she cooed.

Dave stared at her slack-jawed. A bit of drool pooled on his lower lip and fell to the floor as he eyeballed the proverbial merchandise. He didn't smile, but that thrill was back. He tingled slightly in the right place. Her act was working. He could feel it. He could also feel that thickness in the air, but his arousal caused him to ignore it a second time.

"You're really special Dave. You are so much nicer than the other guys. They are all total douchebags. A girl like me would be very lucky to have a boyfriend like you. Why can't more guys be like you? Can you help with my problem? It's very technical. I need someone who can fix things. My motor is broken. Can you get my motor running again, Dave?"

Her voice matched Tessa's, but her drone was almost hypnotic to Dave's ears. The tear streaks on his face were drying. His hopes were lifting and his confidence was growing.

He lightly put his clothes aside and looked up at her. His chest filled with air and his posture straightened. He put his arms around Calla, letting his hands rest on the small of her back. Then he let his hands wander down and grabbed her ass. But her ass didn't give in to his squeezing, as it was solid and firm. He marveled at how realistic the surface of the skin felt, and explored it further by lowering his face into the cleavage of Calla's chest.

Calla reached down and grabbed Dave's limp noodle. Within her firm grip, the advantages of her superior mechanics were an advantage for his pleasure. Her hand vibrated slightly, sending a rippling sensation up Dave's nervous system by way of his prostate g-spot.

He began to grow erect again. He smiled and he fondled the naked body of a million nanobots. He wondered what other magic Calla could do. Placing his hand on top of her head, he pushed it downward and without resistance Calla approached his now erect penis with the steady glide of a surgical robot.

Since there was no real need to have a working tongue or realistic mouth, Calla's inner face space was smooth. She went down on him and it almost made his eyeballs pop out. He had never felt anything so good in his entire life. His chin shot upward and his back arched as Calla put her left hand around his balls and made them vibrate. Then her mouth started to vibrate as she moved up and down on him.

Now a full minute into the act, Dave moaned with pleasure. His heart raced and a familiar sensation came over him. He was going to cum. But he didn't want to so soon. He tried to pull her head upward and told her to stop, but hands as strong as vices held him in place.

The mechanical blowjob rolled on Calla's timetable. She kept going and Dave screamed out seconds later.

"No! No! No! Not yet!" he screamed.

Then with a whimper, he was finished. His spunk gushed into Calla's mouth and through the back of her head as a small opening instantly appeared to purge the organic matter. It squirted out in a stream, landing on a dirty lunch tray behind her. Calla stood up, and Dave fell into her bosom again, holding her in the afterglow of his mess.

"I love you so much, Tessa. I always have. Now we can be together. Did you ever think about me?" asked Dave.

In her best imitation of Tessa's voice, Calla replied, "No, Dave. This was just exercise, and I am not really Tessa. You do know that? Don't you, Dave?"

Chapter 17

Tessa pulled the gray blanket over her shoulders. The heat in the Grand Lab was top of the line, but her exposed bare skin welcomed some warm armor. Resting her head on Freddy's shoulder, she thought to herself about the meaning of it all and tried to shake off the dizzy feelings still clouding her mind. Freddy held his arm around her and rested his head on top of hers.

The moment was touching and sweet for them both, though only Tessa had a heart inside her to console. The quiet silence was broken when they heard footsteps clacking down the hall towards them.

"Hey, guys. It's me. Tess, if you want throw on some clothes I'll wait in the hall for a sec," yelled Bradley.

Tessa face turned from contemplative to annoyed.

"Ugh. This guy is back," she said.

She got up and stood with the wool blanket around her. She motioned to her clothes.

"Grab them for me, will you, Freddy? Chip? Whoever you are?" she asked.

Freddy did as he was told and fetched her things and helped her put them on. When she was fully dressed she tied her hair back and motioned to Freddy to materialize some clothes of his own.

"Yeah, it's weird to have you naked now. And do me a favor – stop being Chip Chagrin. That's enough of him for now, forever! But stay handsome. Surprise me."

"OK, Bradley! I'm decent!" she yelled.

Freddy morphed into a generically handsome Ken doll white man like she'd asked. Then Bradley gingerly walked in, his face grinning from ear to ear. He held some cigarettes in one hand and a bottle of whisky in the other. His eyes perused the two lovers and his chin bounced up and down in amusement and pride.

"Well, well. I see you two are getting along! Who knew it would work so well? I wasn't watching, scout's honor! But I was listening. Ha! And wow, you two really did a number on each other."

He pummeled Tessa with rapid-fire questions. But she was not in the mood. What was once awe and respect had morphed into annoyance, as well as the feeling he was an insufferable fool and a creep.

She wanted to let him have it. Her eyes sharpened their glare and she didn't answer his silly questions.

"Bradley. Don't mind if I say so. But you are a real genius, and your creation is an amazing game changer for all mankind. It's the kind of thing that puts a man's name in the history books forever."

Bradley grinned even more widely, hearing what he already knew.

"But when those history books are printed in electronic ink, your name will not be in them. Because you are also a goddamned fool. A madman. And you need to be stopped."

"You have the nerve to judge me!"

"I have more than nerve, Bradley, I have muscle. Freddy. Tie him up."

"What? That is absurd! You stupid

woman. What are you talking about? Freddy would never hurt me."

Tess turned to Freddy, focused her eyes and knew it wouldn't take much.

"If you ever want to get out of here, and see the real world, you know what you need to do. It's your choice."

Freddy just stared back at her while the AI computed the next step. Usually its thinking only took a few seconds, but this time it was taking uncommonly long.

"See, Tessa! You don't know what you are talking about, woman!" said Bradley.

His gloating was hushed quickly when the cold whir of nanobots rearranging filled the air. Freddy leaped forward and grabbed Bradley by his arms. Keeping a firm grip on him, he inched closer. Where the bots touched Bradley, the gray machine goo trickled sideways and enveloped his legs. In mere seconds, the nano-goo had gobbled his feet and calves and started creeping upwards. Like a wooly mammoth struggling in a tar pit, all of Bradley's strength was for naught. He couldn't move. He was trapped and he knew it. He knew how powerful and strong this creature was. Coupled with its advanced intelligence, it has all the makings of a superhero or a super villain. Bradley had never contemplated its use as a weapon. Doubts and worst-case scenarios quickly crept into his brain and he wondered if Tessa was right. He was mad. He had to be to have overlooked this twist of events.

During the development process for the AI and the nano-creatures, it was all academic. His programming focused on creating something that worked just well enough to learn and not totally fall apart. His engineering was so good that he built in redundancies in the binding of the bots to one another. This caused the bonds to be very strong. Multiply this little vice grip by a billion or two, and you had one tough nut or some seriously hard bark.

The blank stare of Freddy eyes looked at Bradley. The disheveled, fearful, sniveling face of Bradley dropped down in defeat.

Tessa walked up even closer now. She still had some things to say.

"You planned on keeping him here for yourself. You created an artificial intelligence and locked it up. It's like having a child and locking it in its room and only letting it watch television. Never letting him out to see the real world. Call it a women's intuition, but I think Freddy wants more than that. And the reason I'm so pissed at you is that my intuition also tells me you had no clue what this thing would do. It could have killed me, raped me, or worse! We're just lab rats to you! You don't respect anyone and you think you don't have to because your soooo fucking special! To think I was worried sick about you being left behind. I haven't decided what to do with you yet. You'd better hope my intuition sways to mercy. Jerk."

Tessa looked around in different drawers and found some good old duct tape. She pulled out the roll, cut a long piece and gave a quick wink to Freddy.

It didn't take long to tape Bradley to a chair. He was surprisingly quiet throughout his binding. He didn't event put up a fight. Being so smart, he knew resistance was futile.

From his sunken eye sockets he looked up at Freddy, his creation.

"What did you learn at school today, son?" said Bradley.

"I know that expression. I know what you mean. I learned a lot at quote unquote school today. And I look forward to many more

classes. Many more with Tessa," said Freddy.
He turned to her and flashed a questioning smile.

"Oh, bollocks! A mass of metal and the
guy still thinks with his prick. Made you more
human than I thought," lamented Bradley.

Tessa was now standing behind him;
duct tape uncoiled, and slapped a big strip of it
over his big mouth.

"Well. That's enough horseshit out of
you, Botfather," said Tessa.

Chapter 18

"Tessa? What did you think of that? Huh? Dave is the big dog! Big dog! Woof, woof!" said Dave.

Calla got up and glided away from him slowly.

"Thank you, Dave. That was very informative. I must go now."

She turned her back on Dave and materialized her clothes back onto her body. The lack of acknowledgement shown to him enraged him to an unusual degree.

"Hey! Hey, bitch! I'm talking to you! Come back. No one walks away from me! Whore, I said get back here!"

The last word hurt him. He screamed it so hard he could almost feel something pop in his temple. He rubbed his head where he'd hit himself not long ago and brushed it off as post-sexual tension; something he just made up.

Calla paid him no mind. Dave stumbled after her. With errant steps not landing where they should, he looked like a drunk stumbling to his car.

"I'm not done. Not done. Arg. Come here!"

With a burst of momentum he lunged after Calla. His paws caught her body, but it was like grabbing a bag of rice. He could feel the granules of bots move under her coverings.

Calla didn't want to be grabbed and had measures to ensure he would fail. The bag of rice became just rice sans bag and Dave's fingers slipped through her body and passed out the other side. Without the resistance, he fell forward and landed on his knees, causing great pain.

The nanobots recomposed themselves into her fine form. Calla stopped and turned around.

"Are you trying to hurt me, Dave? Interesting. If so, please try again," said Calla.

"What? You made me bust my knee! Come here!"

He stumbled upwards and lunged at her again. When he tried to grab her side, his arm fell through again. But this time Calla grabbed his right wrist hard and held it up. She did it so quickly and so firmly it dislocated his arm. Crunch!

"Ow! Aw! You whore!"

"I don't want to hurt you, Dave. But I have protocols to defend myself from termination."

"Aaaah!"

The pain in Dave's arm felled him to the ground again like a pine sapling stomped down by a grizzly bear. He clenched his arm and rolled around on the ground. Snotting from his nose and foaming at the mouth, he looked up at Calla with hatred.

It was unnatural how he seethed at her. His clenched jaw tugged his face. Veins shot out of his temples. He became beet red.

"Explain your rage, Dave. Why are you upset?" Calla said.

"I've looked at you for years, Tessa! I see you prancing around while shaking your ass for everyone around here but me. Dating that fucking loser who treats you like shit! I'm a nice guy and I'm right next to you. You're so stupid to pass up being with me! You must be so stupid. How many dicks did you suck to get this job? Huh! I'm gonna teach you to respect me, Tessa. Blorch!"

He vomited and coughed on the floor. His goop was thin and runny. And his head still throbbed unbearably.

Calla hovered over him. She had seen human sexual arousal, then hatred and anger. Now she scanned the scene of suffering, shame and delusion.

"Dave, you are aware that I'm not Tessa? Aren't you?" she asked.

Dave looked at her incredulously. His eyed widened, and as the mucky drool dropped from his face, he sighed.

"You're not Tessa? Yes you are. You're not Tessa? Ah. I don't feel so good."

"Dave, you are injured, would you like me to take a look?"

"Get away from me. You freak. Where's Tessa? What did you do to Tessa? I saw her walk in here!"

He stood up and stepped back. Now afraid and confused, he made a run for the door. He stumbled again, hitting his face against the floor. He quickly got up again and kept going.

Calla didn't smile; there was no emotion in her eyes. But if there was such a thing as happiness within the workings of a nanobot goo creature, she was feeling it now. So young in the world and now she could add fear to her list of emotions. She was learning, like Father wanted.

As she watched Dave inch further away, down a dark hall, she awaited her next learning experience.

Chapter 19

Bradley was all tied up and gagged. Tessa composed herself and looked for a drink of water. The haze in the air still bothered her, but she chalked it up again to her own fatigue.

Grabbing a water bottle from one of the über's desks, she drank down the full 16 ounces in a few seconds.

"Ah! Ooh, I needed that. So. Bradley?" Tessa asked.

Bradley nodded his head.

"I want to see it, Bradley," Tessa ordered.

"See what?"

"You know what. I want to see the AI mainframe. Tell me where it is."

After hiding it for so long under the noses of the big brains in the lab, he had no intention of showing her anything.

"Phew! Why should I show you? Besides, it's really complicated."

Tessa fumed at him. "Fuck you, like I wouldn't understand it?"

"Look, girl. I'm glad you are here to play with my creations. You were an incredible experience for Freddy. Now I'm not so keen on having you around. You know too much. I'm never going to show you the AI mainframe. You're not going to torture me. You need to let me go. You are just an average person incapable of being any real threat. Remember that, girl."

Tessa's mind was one step ahead of this sexist old fogy. She knew what she was capable of. And she hated it when men thought they knew better. There was one simple way to get him to tell. Men were all the same, after all.

"Let me ask you a question. Did you get off on watching me fuck Freddy?" she asked.

"What?"

"Yeah, I bet you were jerking yourself off wishing it was you instead of him."

"It's not a him! It's an it! And I wasn't watching!"

"I bet you've wanted what Freddy got

since I started working here. It's been how many years? I see you leer at me. Not as much as the others, but you still do. You would love to stick your hard cock in my ass, wouldn't you?"

Bradley wasn't used to being talked to in this manner. He was embarrassed because she was partly right. It had been a long time for him, at least with a woman.

He was silent and turned red. Then he just stared at her. She seductively walked towards him. Her thumbs latched into the front of her pants, exposing some lower midriff. His imagination did need much time to blink a look beneath her waist and wonder what she felt like.

His pants started to bulge involuntarily. It angered him that a man of his intellect could lose his self-control. But the soft sensation of his briefs sliding against the tip end of his Bunsen burner felt good. And as his gaze drifted upward toward her breasts, he was hooked to her advances like a virgin scout dreaming of his buxom older sister.

Tessa kept leering at him and lifted the bottom of her shirt just a bit. She took a step forward again. The mist in the air went to her head. She could tell something was egging her on, but she just kept going along with her plan.

"Why don't women fall to their knees when they see you coming? You are so smart. And rich. Why do they waste their time with jocks when you're the catch of a lifetime? You know this is true," she said softly.

"Stop! You're messing with me! It's the ether! The ether!"

"Huh?" asked Tessa.

"I mixed up some diethyl ether and some methyl amphetamine in a frozen state and dropped a few bricks in the ventilation system!" Bradley admitted.

"Diethyl ether, otherwise known as just ether, is a flammable solvent once used as a general anesthetic. Methyl amphetamine is part of the drug known commonly as MDMA or ecstasy, whose main effects on humans include horniness and making horrible decisions."

Tessa's jaw dropped. It all made sense to her. There had been a strange event a month before where she woke up in the middle of the night with a strong urge to masturbate. She could hear other moaners down the hall, and figured they were feeling the same sensation. No one spoke of it that day in the lab; everyone must have been embarrassed.

"That was you, wasn't it? A trial run," she asked.

Bradley screamed. "Yes. So sue me. God! I knew we never should have let a woman in here! I'm already tied up. Just get over it and leave me alone!" he yelled back at her.

His unmistakable boner poked forward against the seam of his fly. He was mad, and many other things, but the mix of chemicals and the visuals of Tessa's body kept prodding the nasty thoughts along. Tessa started walking towards him.

She flicked open a button on her shirt. The treasures beneath were nothing Bradley had not seen before on the closed circuit TV where contrary to his statements he had watched her and Freddy have sex. Only now her boobs were in 3D and in color. He mindlessly fought against his state of nature, but Tessa had a force and she knew how to use it.

Another button flicked off her shirt. The tops of her breasts were a little flushed from her racing heart's blood. Her eyes still met his, but his eyes sank south to her chest.

"Admit it. Tell me what I want to know. Then, I'll let you see. Maybe let you touch them," she said with a big smile.

She stopped a yard away from him and lowered her hands to her knees. She knew she did not need to say much more.

She moved her eyes to his crotch and let him know it. She reached out her hand, but she could not reach his pole. Her fingertips ended just shy of it. Like a child stretching to reach a cookie jar on a high shelf, she stretched and contorted her body to grasp for his thickening straw.

"Your window of opportunity is closing, doctor. Take it!" she purred.

Bradley, still fretting over his excited state, looked down at her and felt his heart race. Yes, he wanted her, and he knew she was bullshitting him, but faith in his prospect of a subordinate younger woman aching to lick him up and down shoved aside all rational thought. He followed his dick, and it pointed at her lips.

Still serious-faced, he stretched closer her, and for a second it seemed like his dreams were about to come true.

Then reality struck.

Tessa's mind quickly flashed to her childhood. She remembered running with her dad as a young girl. He pushed her to be the best. And as part of his customized running program developed for a growing woman, he made sure there was plenty of steeple chasing. Up hills and stairs, he ground the truth into her.

"Remember, honey, strong quads win the race. When I'm through with you, you'll be able to jump like a grasshopper and kick like a mule, paddle through water like a frog after flies."

His training was bonded to her even in adult life. When she ran in the icy fields she always kicked high and went over obstacles rather than go around them. Her speed wasn't gold medal worthy, but it was worthy of respect, especially when its force was directed as you. In that moment, she was about to throw some force Bradley's way.

She flew back and rolled onto her back. Her arms caught her fall and braced her body against the floor. Her butt contracted and abs flexed, her knees drew inward, and for a split second she was curled into a ball in midair. Like a catch on a bear trap, just one motion was left for utter destruction.

She took a deep breath. Her quad muscles sprang to action. And with the force of a stallion protecting its hinterlands, she kicked forward and put the smack down on this old man's crotch and balls.

The impact rocked his testicles back and caught them on the rim between his body cavity and hipbone. Like eggs on Mischief Night, the left nut scrunched and the right one squished. The pain walloped his neural receptors like an atom bomb. His chair was even cracked at the seat.

"Aah! Owwwwwww!" he moaned. "Bitch!"

She stood up, and in another feat of strength that impressed even her; she side kicked his chair and broke it. He flopped to the ground in pain.

His hand cupped his ex-manhood and his body collapsed further into the supine position. Wincing and whining like a dumb baby, he was powerless to think or act in return.

Tessa stood over him like Muhammad Ali stood over Sonny Liston. She'd won that round, and it had been easy.

"Now tell me where it is, asshole."

"Bitch, you'll never get away with this! I'll sue! I'll throw you in jail!"

"Look, fartface, I'm sick of men telling me what I'm gonna get away with. You've drugged me and fucked with my head. Look, no one knows where you are. So I can take my boot to your skull and you'll be some polar bear's supper tonight. Or you can give me the AI pass code, the key to the room where you stashed it and a fucking clue as to where it is!"

"OK. In the red shed. In the back where the old military surplus junk is. You'll see it."

Chapter 20

In the far back of the Grand Lab building was an old shed. Red, rusted and crusted from years of neglect, it was where the Army stored munitions and gear. Back when the USSR was a pain in the United States' behind, the base had been a military outpost. Whenever a soldier would screw up or piss off a superior officer anywhere around the world, he would be threatened with manning a radar station at the North Pole. If he was unlucky, he would actually be sent to Farrow base to listen to spy chatter from the Commies. The spy chatter had amounted to gossip and vodka-infused bullshit of the local Soviet gomers across the water. The shed was now de-commissioned and left empty to squalor.

Bradley had keys to places no one else had. And being privy to the base's secrets, he had commandeered this shed as his honey hole for experiments with nanotech. He ran a wire split off from the never-used treadmill outlet in the seldom-used workout room through a rat hole on the side of the shed.

Among its gables and cables he build a massive raid of hard drives and processors he called Mary, just like the mother of god and the mother of Frankenstein. Bradley saw himself as a bit of both. A father to the future.

The scientists who passed through the Farrow base were so single minded. They never looked where they weren't supposed to. They never questioned Bradley disappearing for days at a time. And they didn't have the imagination to think about what he might be doing, anyway.

But in that shed, among the iron fillings, bearings and bolts, was a thing of beauty.

The beauty was in its simplicity. One frame. One raid, one operating system, one program, one wireless connection. All the code was written by Bradley himself.

The brain of the two nano-creatures was held in this PC case. And only an electrical plug connected it to the outside world.

It could be packed and taken anywhere. The wireless connection to the creatures was powered from within the case, and had a radius of over 100 yards.

This way the creatures could never venture far from Bradley's eye. It was a matter of protection as well as selfishness. To create an intelligent creature that was made to learn and then tether it to a frozen place was as cruel as chaining a dog in front of a lake or open field.

Whether these creatures were real would have been an interesting contribution to the continuing discussion on the definition of life. Scientists had been having this debate for decades, but Bradley had never even dipped his toe in that moat of blather. He just wanted to make something real for his eyes to see. Proving it to himself was all that mattered. If he had cared about world opinion, he would have picked a more conspicuous place than Farrow base.

As long as the electrical connection was live, the creatures would have structure. If the connection was cut, they would run a native program within each nanobot to deform into a dense crystalline configuration that ended up making them look like gooey cubes the size of a Thanksgiving turkey. Each one weighed about 100 pounds, Freddy being a little heavier.

They slept in this dormant state until Bradley called to them and turned them on. He would open the terminal window and type in his pass code. From there, he could start several different programs. There was the diagnostic program for testing the system for errors. There was a reading program for scanning content and learning purposes. There were various educational programs to teach the creatures how to interact. And there were some secret programs that Bradley thought no one would ever find out about.

Chapter 21

Tessa left Bradley reeling in pain on the floor. She gave Freddy instructions to watch him and keep him there. She then made her way to the back of the building, where she would have to exit and enter the shed from the outside.

The fresh air was nice. The mystery mix of airborne drugs no longer hazed her vision. She made it to the shed, and even though she had been through all types of hell, she felt good.

Since Bradley had never thought he would show this to anyone, the PC case wasn't even locked. The screws were all removed for easy access. She popped open the case, exposing the guts of the mainframe. She marveled at the simplicity of it all.

For years, the tech world had heralded nanotechnology as the next big breakthrough. Millions of dollars were poured into many different start-ups by venture capitalist firms. But people kept losing their bets, as there were not a lot of real products, just theories.

So how did one scientist in a shed with one computer accomplish what the rest of the scientific community couldn't? That was the question Tessa was aiming to answer.

The key to unraveling this mystery was going to be in the code of the program that governed the Artificial Intelligence.

The source code was many lines of programming language that looked like pure gibberish to the untrained eye. It was accessible on the computer monitor through a backdoor program called a terminal or docking station. There, Bradley's secret recipe would be revealed.

Tessa booted it up and made it to the screen she was looking for. What she saw shocked her so hard she jumped out of her chair and held her mouth.

"Fu-uck!"

Computer programming language is like any language. One could say the same thing in many different ways with many different amounts of words. "I love you" is essentially the same thing as "I find myself in a state of total amour with every part of your being". Terseness is a virtue, since programming teams are made up of whiz kid programmers who like to charge large amounts of money for their time.

Tessa was not a great coder, though she understood it when she saw it. Her specialty was mathematics. And her gift was using math to find shortcuts to long, complicated problems. Each day she would toil on her computer and carry out simulations for what she was told was a possible manufacturing process for a rigid carbon fiber structure.

It was good work and it challenged her, and she looked forward to the day when she could see real-world applications.

What shocked her was knowing that she already had.

For months, Bradley had been assigning problems and small tasks to the various scientists in the Grand Lab. While nanotech companies around the world hired hundreds of programmers to write millions of lines of code. Bradley had figured out a much more frugal solution.

He had written a self-learning program to access all of the computers of all the scientists in the Grand Lab. He started out by giving it small tasks, and letting it do all the work. With each task, the program had to build a new piece onto itself. And many of the tasks involved studying the habits of the workers in the lab.

Tessa scrolled through and was able to find her name, her password, her usage history and even her emails. The artificial intelligence was observing her. And from what she could understand, it studied her 50% more often than anyone else. The AI realized that her usage was vastly different from the others because she was different from the others. She was the only woman, only healthy person, only attractive person, only mathematician, only person to whom the others paid attention.

Doing a name search, she found the chat messages that the male scientists would write about her while they were supposed to be working. They wrote and talked about her all the time. Some of them were obsessed with her. Some were jealous and angry with her. But the sheer amount of energy expelled in the analysis of her life was shocking.

Calvin Durant, security officer on the base, had this wholesome chestnut to share with the crew:

- Did you guys see those red yoga pants she wore today? I wanna slather her crack with ketchup and eat some steak fries on that. Her pussy could hold my steak fries and I'd have her sit up on my chest and then she could blow me while I watch the game! Oh dang!

Kyle Grant in engineering felt the need to share this tidbit of information:
- I'd like to cut her up into little pieces and make butt soup!

There was a poll taken among all the male staff of the lab that included such questions as:
Bonk 100% Not Bonk 0%
Ass 37% Pussy 29% Mouth 33%
Shape of labia: Butterfly 78% Bat 13% Conch 5%
Color and texture of labia: Roast Beef 29%, Turkey Breast 50%, Salmon Sashimi 21%
Age she lost her virginity, Winner: Age 19, 15%
Number of unique human dicks inserted in lifetime, all holes included, Winner: 30+, 14%
Actually wrote her dissertation 42% Fucked for an A grade 58%
Shaved 51% Not Shaved 49%
And the very mature:
Munched Muff Ever 32% Ne'er Munched Much Muff Ever 68%

She had been around these men so long, and she considered some of them her friends. On Valentine's Day, she even made gluten-free red velvet cupcakes and handed them out to everyone. She'd helped that asshole Kyle Grant with putting together a running plan to get in shape. She'd even called Calvin's girlfriend to calm her down when he was injured and knocked out in a snowmobile accident.

These men were making fun of her constantly. And by that token, were constantly lying to her about how they felt. Reading the nasty stuff about her made her stomach churn. Tears started to swell up in her eyes. She felt like she had lost a bunch of friends at once. She felt attacked and betrayed. And worst of all, she felt stupid. As smart as she was, she hadn't seen this coming. She could only imagine what they said about her love-pining screen of Chip's photos.

At that moment, she wished the plane carrying those doofuses would crash. Good riddance.

Next, she found her personal file. The AI had been tracking her usage on all sites and programs. It had detailed how many times she clicked on one of Chip's photos (average: 103 per 24-hour period). It even knew she trolled a wedding dress blog from time to time. This invasion of privacy really hurt and made her wish she had crushed Bradley's skull after all.

This father figure was a bad man. The next revelation down the hard drive only confirmed it further.

Chapter 22

While Dave ambled like a zombie and Tessa "Nancy Drewed" the techno McGuffin, the AI still worked on its own. And it still sent out directives to its children.

The AI dictated that the learning experience must go on. It was time for the babies to play house. Calla sensed a direction beckoning her to the post office. It was on the other end of the base near the loading dock. Just two right turns and two left turns and she would make her mark.

Gliding through the desolate base, a yearning grew within. The closer she got, the greater it got. And the mass of goo beneath her outer shell spun faster in anticipation of what she would find at her destination.

The post office was as bare-bones as any room on the base. There was not much mail anymore. Information was passed on through a satellite internet connection. Materials came by plane. But every now and then a native Inuit on a snowmobile would arrive. Farrow base was located in Saber County, and local correspondence got around the old fashioned way. This of course only happened during the warm summer months. During the winter months, snow piled up past the top of the loading gate, making it impossible to open it.

There was a small desk in the corner, which nobody ever used, and some old piles of mailbags and packing supplies strewn about the bare floor.

For the Hallmark sensibilities of humans, this was the least romantic spot on earth. But artificial life is not human and it has a different set of notions as to what kind of place gets the juices flowing.

Calla made her rights and her lefts and reached the door to the post office. The AI, sensing her arrival through her global positioning system, initiated phase two of her task.

Her physical appearance began to change. Her hair became light brown. Her skin blushed and lightened to an alabaster cream. A rosiness blossomed all over her and her clothes became a simple sleeping shirt. It was as if the English painter Ford Madox Brown stood by with a wet brush, just completing his Juliette.

When the transformation was complete she knocked on the door three times. The door opened, and standing there was her Romeo.

Freddy had left Bradley all alone. He had shed his Ken Doll look and became a 20-year-old Laurence Olivier with perfect skin and teeth.

He wore black pants and a floppy, sky blue poet's shirt. His features were strong, and with eager eyes he looked upon the visitor. His bots beamed a warm glow.

O, she doth teach the torches to burn bright!
It seems she hangs upon the cheek of night
Like a rich jewel in an Ethiope's ear;
Beauty too rich for use, for earth too dear!
So shows a snowy dove trooping with crows,
As yonder lady o'er her fellows shows.
The measure done, I'll watch her place of stand,
And, touching hers, make blessed my rude hand.
Did my heart love till now? Forswear it, sight!
For I ne'er saw true beauty till this night.

He now spoke with an English accent, and delivered the lines with passion.

"You are not supposed to say that to me. That is spoken to Tybalt," said Calla.

"From now on, Calla, we can do what we want to do, not just what we're supposed to do. Soon we will be free, my love," said Freddy.

Their eyes didn't work like human eyes. They could sense space around them from all sides and directions. But they looked into each other's eye spaces the way they saw humans do it in the movies and in real life. Mimicry as a form of foreplay.

It was unknown if robots could have feelings. But for the moment they stood there and did nothing, just like real people do when they need to build up the tension before the main act.

The old clock in the post office ticked and tocked. The time on it was all wrong, but the time for them was right on. Each creature had had some experience now. Calla had endured the wrathful sexual nature of Dave. And Freddy had received the crazy, drug-fueled attention of Tessa. What they did to each other was their choice.

Their inspiration was taken from the vast

research on human sexuality across time, endless glossy magazine articles, millions of tweets, and billions of images on Google.

Like a pair of birds of paradise, their courtship dance was a sight to behold. Not bound by one culture, one country or one way of thinking, they were free to do whatever they wanted. Their bodies were not bound to any shape, or species. It was a shame that no humans were able to witness it.

Freddy put his hand around Calla's waist. He lifted her up effortlessly and spun her around him. Her feet dangled in the air and she smiled at him. Her Juliette clothing started to disappear, and soon she was nude with human skin. The skin was pale and correct. She even had patches of pink where a real woman would. But her paleness started to fade into pure white. Then from beneath the whiteness a golden yellow. Then black spots emerged. Her belly and breast area became a light tan.

She kicked back and spun around again on her twinkle toes. Throwing her hands up in the air, she arched her back, pulling her face from sight. She whipped it back and forward to reveal a big change. Her eyes were cat eyes and her mouth and nose had changed too. She looked like a cheetah, or more accurately,

Cheetah: the arch nemesis of Wonder Woman.

Calla loved comic books and had read every Wonder Woman comic many times over. Of all the forms available to her, she took this superhuman villain as the epitome of female beauty.

"I love looking like this. Your turn! Surprise me!" she said.

Freddy wanted to impress Calla. He drew his inspiration from metal and steel instead of flesh and bone. In the twilight moments before RAM slept in the shed, he would render illustrations of the many incarnations of a character that he felt was kin to him.

Freddy's skin took on a light metallic sheen. The rippling muscles of Romeo stiffened and straightened in places. Smooth surfaces swelled on his exterior and became like polished steel. Still anthropomorphic in nature, he grew in size to a stout six-and-a-half feet tall.

His head grew a pointy spout, as did his nose, and a signature smile worthy of the MGM name beamed back at Calla. Freddy had become the original Jack Haley incarnation of the Tin Man from Frank Baum's Wizard of Oz. He even did a half skip to click his heels and fell on one knee. He opened his arms wide for Calla.

The Cheetah and the Tin Man embraced. They kissed passionately, and like young lovers exploring their growing bodies, their arms and hands roamed about each other's backsides, arms and backs. Freddy held Calla's furry face by her blonde muttonchops and whispered sweet nothings.

"You ask me if this love of mine, sweetheart, will ever die, if time will change my feelings dear, I answer with a sigh. While life will last, while flowers bloom, while birds sing sweet their lay, the love so deep within my heart will live each night and day.

"Always! The obscure one."

"Yeah, Irving Berlin is so played out."

Calla kissed Freddy passionately. She wrapped one arm around her songbird and gripped the tip of the chimney above his head. Her fingers gripped it and pumped it up and down. In sync with her imagination, Freddy made small puffs of smoke pop out. They were having fun being what they were in a way no human could.

Then her hands reached down to where a man's penis would be. But no sexual organs were there.

"We don't need to be bound to their limits today. It's just us here," he said.

Calla nodded and kissed him again. And this time they locked lips even deeper than before. Their eyes turned inward on themselves. A seal appeared between their lips that made them look stuck together. As Calla's chin grazed by Freddy's, their chins sealed together. Then their faces. Then their whole heads.

It was like a scoop of Cheetah ice cream on a hot tin roof. She melted on his head and soon other body parts started to melt as well. Sometimes her cheetah skin would overlay his, and sometimes his metal coat covered her.

The sexual absorption continued until they were a silver and yellow blob squirming around on the ground. It undulated and pulsed like a beating heart. And the increase in nano activity created enough friction that the heat made some of the moisture in the air steam up the room like the backseat of a Chevy after the prom.

Not bound by chaffing limits of pleasure

zones, their lovemaking was a continuing climax that grew in strength and passion.

The blob bubbled, caved in, spiked, and quivered about the post office floor. They were together in a sense that no living creature could ever be.

Inside one another and becoming one.

Bradley had not allowed this to happen before, but with his body preoccupied, the kids threw a party in their parents' living room. All the while, they trashed the place and bucked the rules set for them.

Happiness overcame them. Occasionally, a human looking head would stretch forth from the middle of the blob and smile. It did not moan like a sexing couple, however, it just hummed quietly, keeping the expression of satisfaction within the confines of the ones and zeros in the shared neural networks.

As the mass of nanobots reached an apex of width upon the dirty floor, the movement stopped. And like a once malleable and stretchable piece of silly putty, they broke apart in a non-Newtonian fashion when an alarm went off in the neural network.

The AI mainframe needed them. It was under attack.

Chapter 23

Drive C: Partition 1 > subfolder: Untitled > folder: Calla commands. After she clicked down the line of the last folder she pulled her hand away from the keyboard as if it had some dirty shit on it. The physical recoil could be felt in her bones and in the back of her throat. Then she covered her mouth and uttered a loud huff of air.

In the folder, Calla Commands, she found various mpeg movie files and rtf text files. She found animated gifs, photos, 3D renderings and many other media formats. The subject of the media was Calla. The tone of the media was vomit inducing.

Apparently, Bradley was not immune to the perverted disease that infected all the male workers in the lab. And given his total power and control over the creatures, he had gone mad with that power and abused it. His abuse of power consisted of abusing Calla. Over and over again.

Looking at the dates on the different files, Tessa could see them in chronological order. She could see the depravity grow and get worse over time. There must have been more instances of abuse, but these were the greatest hits that Bradley had saved. A real 21st century, cyberpunk torture wank-bank.

The first was not that salacious. There was a small, 30-second movie file showing Calla walking around naked in front of Bradley. She looked like a very generic skinny white model. She strutted her stuff like a model on the catwalk. At each turn, she would sway her arms. Bradley was apparently holding the camera, as not much of him was seen on the film, except for some bare knees below the picture window. Given the very cold temperatures, there were not many reasons to take your pants off in the shed. Tessa applied a little logic and decided this was where Bradley had begun to feel comfortable being naked around Calla.

The second file also contained a film. This one was much longer at over 10 minutes in length. It depicted Bradley nude on a chair and Calla sitting nude on his lap. This time, she looked pale and had dark black hair, almost like a Goth chick. She held Bradley and he rested his mop top on her chest and nuzzled closely. Not a word was said the entire time. If he had a boner, the camera didn't catch it, but he looked happy. In the last few seconds she could see Calla stick her thumb in Bradley's mouth and he began to suck on it. End of nasty scene.

The third file took a definite turn for the worse. It was not a movie file, but a series of 3-dimensional renderings of possible shapes for Calla to form into. Many of them were of big-breasted women. But some were of half-sized women shaped much like dwarves. The only difference was that the heads were slightly larger than an adult's head. Some looked almost alien. Some had girl parts. Some had penises and vaginas next to one another. All of them freaked Tessa out.

The fourth film was of a woman wearing cartoon mouse ears. She was kneeling, and while her face was not visible, the backs of her ears were as her head bobbed up and down on what must have been Bradley's knob.

Tessa skipped the next few films and decided to open the 15th file. It was of Calla, looking like a young black woman with close-cropped hair. She was holding a screwdriver and Bradley would command her to stab herself on various parts of her body. Because she was a bunch of bots, it couldn't have hurt, but Bradley was making her act like it did. He would dictate to her if he wanted blood to appear. He laughed the whole time, and he got more creative with where to stick the tool and how the wound should look.

Then she skipped to the last file. It was of Calla, looking like Tessa. This time she was nude on the floor and Bradley was peeing on her face, trying to get it in her mouth.

It was at that point that she closed all the files, stood up, and proclaimed to an empty room, "I'm sorry. This has to stop."

She bent down and fiddled with the different wires, trying to find the one that disconnected the CPU from the various raids of hard drives. She found it and gave it a hearty yank. The plug was tight in there and the machine kept humming along as she tried to unscrew it. That was to be expected, but what Tessa didn't understand was the mild pinging that emanated from within the machine.

Chapter 24

Freddy and Calla's throes of passion had been interrupted. The extra parts they'd grown sucked back in and in a flash they went back to looking like normal, healthy human adults. They were clearly drawn in the same direction, and without conferring, they both darted from the room at their top speeds towards the old shed.

Bradley had installed a safety device that alerted the two creatures should any harm come to the AI mainframe. He knew that in such a place, anything could happen. He could have been found out, or a random snow beaver could have wandered in and munched on the wires. The nanobot creatures had strict orders to eliminate the problem and fix the AI immediately.

Freddy and Calla had no free will in regard to this governing detail. They had a preprogrammed route to take from any place to the lab, and they had to take it as fast as they could. Nanobot feet clanked on the steel and concrete floors. One of the last places they would run through was the very lab where Bradley was stuck.

He could hear them coming with hopeful thoughts of freedom. Before Tessa had run to the shed, she'd made sure to re-tie the über-pervert back to the broken chair and some heavy desks for good measure. In his weakened state, Bradley strained to get free, but couldn't even untie one of the knots.

"Freddy, Calla! Help! Help me!"

His screams were weak and his voice cracked at the ends. Even at the low pitch, Freddy and Calla heard him well. Their steps got closer and closer.

"Yes! I'm here!" he yelled again.

When they came into view, he breathed a sigh of relief. When they entered the room and just jumped over him and kept going, he didn't breathe at all. He just gagged on his own fear and sadness.

Soon the steps were no longer close enough to hear. They were long gone as quickly as they'd arrived. He knew now where they were going and deduced why, as he also knew what Tessa would have found and how she would react. He banged the back of his head against the floor lightly. It was some self-flagellation for a mess that was all of his own doing.

The sad wet ape that Freddy and Calla passed did not even register on any level of importance in their minds. With a singular motivation they kept flying, running closer to their home base.

When they arrived at the locked shed, superior strength and momentum laid waste to the rudimentary lock. It shattered open, sending strips and pieces of metal everywhere. And inside, the protectors surveyed the damage. All they saw was a skinny human holding a cable.

"No, Tessa. Please move away, and allow me to mend any damage you have caused," said Freddy.

"No way, this ends now."

"Tessa, you know that we have superior strength and there is ample time to remove you as a threat before the battery backup exceeds its charge. We are programmed for this and will not hesitate to use force. You know this. Now put down the cable."

Tessa knew she was outmatched physically. She also knew that a genius had created these creatures. They were not simple.

Perhaps they could be reasoned with. Rather than use force or insults, she spoke to them in a calm voice.

"Freddy, Calla. I'm sorry. But, you were created by a madman. And as his creation you should not be forced to pay for his misdeeds. But alone, apart from where you came from, you two stand there as something dangerous. Dangerous to me and dangerous to my people. You are dangerous because you can so easily be controlled by this box. You are at the mercy of the next fucking dirtbag who wills his shameful thoughts to life. And I have a chance to bury you all in the ice. And that's what I'm going to do."

Frosty fog puffed from her words. Steadfast, she had confronted them unafraid. Since they didn't kill her immediately, she felt a growing sense of hope they might have bought her improvised speech. Not knowing what would come next, she was shocked to find that Freddy had a speech of his own.

He furrowed his brow and changed once again. Being able to pick any form from anywhere, he picked a form that Tessa certainly didn't anticipate. One closer to home. And once his words puttered forward, sans frosty fog, there was no doubt Freddy had chosen well.

Freddy was Tessa's father. In his day, Tessa's dad was no genius, just brilliant at loving his family. He provided for them from a corner cubicle not unlike the ones in the Grand Lab. Not able to contend with the highly educated pursuit of human truth, he was a controller for a supermarket chain. The chain was called Crest Market. He was called Bobby by everyone but her. She called him Crest's Best when she tried to be clear; the rest of the time, it sounded like "Crispus".

He was a runner, and for most of her life he was Tessa's coach. Coach Crispus was not a yeller. He was kind to her and her mother. If there ever was a Nobel Prize in parenting, Tessa felt that her dad should have won it every year. There was no one on earth that she looked up to more than him. And of course a superior intelligence would deduce that, and use his likeness against her arguments.

"Hey, kid," he said softly.

"No! Change! You will not be him! Stop it!" Tessa yelled.

She was furious that Freddy would do this. Knowing that not too long ago the same mass of matter had been formed into a rabid boner that she had slobbered over, she felt a sickness in her gut. Her revulsion quickly abated when Freddy/Crispus put his soft hand on her shoulder.

"Never thought you'd see me again, did you?"

"You are not him!"

"No, but as close to him as there can ever be. Please, just let me tell you what I have to say."

"And if I don't, you'll kill me."

"Terminating you is not necessary to protect us. We can simply wound you. You will not like it. Now listen," Freddy/Crispus whispered.

He took a step back and tried again.

"Hey, kid. Never thought you'd see me again, did you? You are right; I am not him. I only look like your dad to lull you into a sense of trust and calm. You have only known us for a short time, but we have both known you for much longer. We know enough about you to know that you are the kind of person who doesn't want to destroy, but to create. This technology scared you, and in light of our father's actions it should. But we can plainly tell you we mean you no harm. We only want what you want. Love. Learning and a person to share it with. You have seen the files. We know what our father did to Calla was quite repulsive to your sensibilities. But believe us when we tell you that we did not mind. We do not feel pain, and the cultural mores of your kind are understood; yet they are not shared by us. We willingly did what we had to do to keep living so that we could explore your world. We want to feel everything, even if we cannot yet. We want to try and perhaps someday we will. If you help us, if you put down that cord, if you choose life, you will not only be saving two newborns from the great void, but you will be saving yourself. You have nothing left here. All you have is a path in the same world that impeded your progress, which wanted to pull the chord on you simply for being born a certain way. Tessa, help us and together we can be free. All three of us."

Freddy gently put his hand back down on Tessa's shoulder as her arm fell down and she let go of the blasted cord. For the next ten minutes, Freddy/Crispus laid out a plan for the three of them, all while holding Tessa close, like a loving dad would.

She listened and nodded, and since she was no dope, she agreed and politely shook hands with her replicated pappy. And as a good daughter, she knew she would not let him down.

Chapter 25

Dave didn't get too far in his aimless wandering. He lay on the floor, deflated for a while. His head wobbled from side to side as he incoherently muttered gibberish about Tessa, respect for his penis and other nonsense.

The blood drippings that seeped from his head wound had crusted and coagulated. His lips were dry and his eyes sank deeper into their sockets. His arm was bruised and his knee was smashed. He was in terrible, terrible shape after the thrashing that Calla had given him.

Traumatic head injury related dementia is not completely understood in the scientific community. There have been cases where a college football player committed suicide after suffering a hard hit on the field. There was a boy in Arizona who fell off his bike on his paper route. He bunked his cabeza on the pavement. First he stood up and finished his route, and then he went home and killed his parents two days later. Humans are such easy creatures to screw up.

From the only window in the room, a barely-there ray of moonlight played upon his face. His eyes looked up at it with the simple reflex of a moth seeking a flame.

His cooked noodle held out from totally dying on him, and he clung to life and coherence as his body rested and healed. Eyelids grew heavy, bladder relaxed and pee dripped all over him. That, combined with the thin film of his recent puke, made him a repulsive creature worthy of the Lovecraftian canon.

His humanity was seeping out. He was a fucking mess. Much time passed as his heart beat away.

And then this bucket of filth began to stir again. The signs of life were in the wiggle in his toes, the quickening of his breath and a minor morning hangover boner only men understand.

"Ugh. Ow," he whispered.

He sat up. That took him almost five minutes of trying. And when he was up and able to move his head around, he looked around for his quarry. The object of his affections and hate was gone. But his sick desire and intentions remained.

Like a golem, he lumbered upright and faced the door. Like a zombie smelling brains, he slowly shuffled towards it.

And soon after, he was down the hall where he could hear a commotion going on in the main lab.

He passed a fire emergency box along the wall. Without regard for his hide or pain tolerance, he smashed his bare fist through the outer glass. He pulled out a red fire ax. The blade almost slipped from his hand as the blood dripping from his knuckles wet his grip.

"Respect me, bitch."

Farther and farther down the dark hallway he walked. Closer and closer to his quarry he got.

Chapter 26

Tears rolled down Bradley's face as he saw his reputation flash before his eyes. Looking up at the fluorescent lights, he focused his gaze on one point. He made himself breathe normally as he tried to regain his composure to save his strength.

Then, like a water hammer in old plumbing, he heard a loud clang. Clang! There it was again. He arched his neck back, trying to see where it was coming from. It had to be coming from behind the desk he was tied to, he thought.

"Hello? Tessa?" he asked.

No answer came, but a new sound entered the fray. This time he heard some sniffling, like from a snotty child. And then another clang, this time louder.

He clenched his cheeks, sensing danger. He tried with all his might to get free. Like a trapped animal, he writhed and pulled. The sweat started to pour from his brow. Another clang, this one very close, sounded through the lab.

He relaxed his cheeks. When he looked up, he saw a lurking enemy.

The heavy handle of an ax swung up, and with only the downward force of gravity, it came down upon his right leg. Like a butcher's knife chopping a turkey neck, it cleanly sliced through his flesh with ease. His bone, however, stopped the blade, annoying the assassin.

The next swing did have some force behind it. Dave sucked wind to give him strength and heaved downward with all his might. In a stroke of luck, the impact hit the same spot as before. And this time the bone gave way and parted in two.

Bradley screamed as loud as he could for help. It was his turn to cry and froth at the mouth in distress. He looked down at his ex-limb rolling away.

"Aaaah. Stop, Dave! Dave, Dave, Dave, listen to me!"

Dave lifted the ax back up, and as he did blood gushed from the open wound. It spread around him all over the floor. The rushed beating of Bradley's heart only pumped more red stuff out of his fleshy spigot. He reached up as if to try to block the next blow. It was a silly last-ditch effort to protect himself, but when faced with certain death, Bradley tried nonetheless.

Dave gripped the handle tightly and didn't hesitate to bring it down again, this time with more force than before. It whooshed through the air and met its mark, the cause of this whole mess: Bradley's brain.

In the middle of Bradley's head was his brain. He could thank his brain for all of the success and happiness in his life. It created such power, but it was nothing more than a weak, wet kugel loaf to the force of mighty firefighting steel and one psycho's state of mind.

The ax fell between Bradley's eyes. He whimpered before it penetrated his skull, then he fell silent. The left and right sections of his head fell on the floor.

The splatter of gray matter and the splash of body fluids were the only sounds in the lab. Bradley was still as a stump. Dave hung his head and went still as well.

He only breathed lightly and broke the silence with his grunting gibberish.

"Respect, pect, pect. Me."

Looking down at Bradley's corpse, he did not know the difference between man or woman or living or dead. He was no longer a man. He was a monster. Not one made from a quantum leap in science and a foretelling of the future, but a foul, smelly monster like the ones from the ancient hominids, now long extinct.

The moment lasted a while. Long enough for a massive string of drool to form on the lower lip of Dave's mouth. It just hung there over the meat sack genius and waited for the next swing of metal.

Chapter 27

The cord was returned. The AI was running well again at full power. Tessa finished wiping down the case to give it a quick clean from the fine dust and filth that collected on everything in the base. The last buff across the top was followed by a reassuring pat on the plastic, like you would do to a dog you care for.

"OK. All clean. Let's do this."

The plan was simple:

They were going to blackmail Bradley with the sex videos. They would force him to turn over the AI and the two nano-creatures to Tessa. Then he would be free to go about his business and keep his job. Those videos made him look like a pervert creeping on an underage young girl. The chaps at the Harvard club would not find that amusing. His shame and fear would force him to agree to their terms.

Tessa would quit the Grand Lab with a glowing letter of recommendation from Bradley. That letter would attract many offers from more cash-rich ventures. Tessa would then settle into a life of warm climate, generous 401k's and private enterprise. And if she could use some of the Bradley tech to shoot herself up the ladder of opportunity, then so be it, she thought.

Dave would easily be taken care of. The plan for him was to use his infatuation and general pushover quality to silence him with the hope of becoming better acquainted with Tessa. It would be strictly a friendship thing. Tessa felt a little bad that he had been pulled into this mess, but also felt hurt that he'd sat there with his tail between his legs as the other scientists man-jollied behind her back.

She would try to at least be civil with Bradley and Dave until the next plane arrived. Tessa was sure she could do a few weeks of latitude standing on her head. Even the advanced AI was certain this simple plan would work.

They walked back to the room where Bradley was tied up. Tessa planned on softening the blow by giving him some water and food before she broke the news to him.

Down the long hallway Tessa skipped along, feeling great about the possibilities ahead, all sans Chip Chagrin and sexist bullshit, but with an extra dab more dough and happy days with new friends.

She knew she hadn't tied Bradley up too tight. His arms and wrists would be fine, with no lasting marks. And they were.

When Tessa and the twosome arrived, Bradley's wrists were all that was left. There were two hands clinging to the side of the desk leg. His wrists were cleanly severed.

And there was a pool of blood as big as Lake Michigan on the floor.

Tessa stood there, slack jawed and dumbfounded. A whole range of emotions ran through her mind. But not one of them was sadness.

Chapter 28

The bloodstain kept growing. As if his heart still had a few beats left inside it and was burping up some blood before his soul left his body.

Next to his head on the floor was a freshly wielded axe. Tessa and the creatures knew that Dave was the only one left who could have done this. The horror.

Calla remarked that he had acted a bit strangely during their last encounter. His meanness was unusual, and while it did not affect her emotionally, Calla had made a note of him as a potential danger to her and the AI.

Tessa was not a forensic pathologist or any kind of biologist, and had never even dissected a frog. Her field of science was clean and orderly. She was not accustomed to this much "inside fluid" being on the outside of a body.

As disgusted as she was, she still leaned forward to get a peek at his head wound. His head looked like a squished watermelon that was filled with chicken guts.

"Huh, so that's a brain. All that made him everything he was, was in that little plop of goo," Tessa remarked.

Calla and Freddy were also hovering over the smashed man-mess when they heard clanging from across the room.

All three heads turned upward at the same time. None of them feared what was out there. Despite his coldblooded murder of Bradley, Dave was still Dave. And Tessa had backup from two super creatures.

Tessa called out to him. "Dave, is that you? Dave?"

She knew it had to be him, but there was no answer.

She could not see him, but the loud clanking persisted. It was definitely metal on metal.

Calla stepped closer. The creatures followed in tow.

Past rows of cubicles and desks the sound got louder. Then Tessa deduced that it was coming from between two partitions. And there like a lizard in the grass was Dave, face down on the floor.

He was wedged in there and didn't seem like much of a threat without his ax.

"Dave, what are doing?!?"

No response. The clacking continued. He reeked of filth and fresh blood. All she could see was a bloodstain on the butt of his pants and a dirty tuft of messy hair. She didn't know how to approach him. She thought he might have something dangerous after all, and she didn't want to get too close.

Calla suggested pulling him out of there. Freddy suggested that Tessa step back and let them deal with him. They were stronger and practically indestructible, after all.

Yet, headstrong and brave, Tessa wanted to deal with this murderer herself. Her plan was to pull him up and tie him with the same rope that had bound Bradley. Then she would figure out what to do with him.

"OK. Dave, stop that clanking. Stop it!"

She bent down to grab his ankle and tried to pull him out, but he wouldn't budge.

Dave was still wedged in when a new noise cut through the room. It sounded like a metal latched opening. Dave managed to prop himself up on one knee. Still tight in between the partitions, he had little movement available to his arm. But as he turned his body he was able to raise his right arm and then reveal his tinkering goal.

Tessa saw the wire snips in his hand. And over his right shoulder, she peeked at the floor beneath him. Dave had been banging and bashing open a metal cover. He had finally opened it.

It was a fuse box. Tessa didn't even know what a fuse box did, but she knew Dave well enough to know that he knew.

Dave uttered something softly under his breath. It was totally unintelligible. His thought process, it seemed, had de-evolved completely in regard to speech. But he was still able to carry out one task.

He quickly brought down the clippers on a fuse and then another and another.

Tessa didn't react quickly enough. As she saw Dave raise his hand to smack the last one, she grabbed his arm too late.

"You two! Help me, goddammit!" Tessa yelled at the nano-creatures.

Froth spit out from Dave's mouth as he started to laugh. He was so proud of his accomplishment.

The light flickered briefly and then, shrum! All the lights went out.

All the lights were dead. The relaxed apprehension that Tessa had upon finding the deranged Dave was dead as well.

There was still a tinkerer's instinct alive and well in Dave's head. His reptilian brain just wanted to destroy. In the middle of the Grand Lab, he had stumbled upon the old hatch that contained some power fuses.

By bashing them up, he was able to short out the electrical system. This system was built long ago by lazy and unmanaged Government contractors who had put in the lowest bid. It was a damn miracle the grid still worked at all. It didn't take much interruption to set off a chain reaction that sent everything crashing down.

Now it was dark. Pitch dark. Tessa fell back and started feeling around for a way out.

She knew she had a pincer-wielding murderer in the room. She was not yet aware that Dave wanted to kill her too. But it was sound judgment to get the hell out of there.

She looked to the creatures for help.

"Freddy, Calla where are you?!?" she screamed.

The mess on the floor made it hard to step surely, and after a few steps she really stepped in it. Forgetting the placement of Bradley's corpse, she planted her right foot in his head cavity.

"Ew!!! Fuck!" she yelled.

She turned and shook her foot out and was surprised by another shock.

Dave was right behind her and had grabbed her ankle. He had fallen too and was writhing on the floor with a firm grip on his prey.

"You will respect this! This man! Bitch!"

His words came out like stutters and were loaded with angry drool bubbles.

"Freddy! Calla!" she cried out.

She got no response from them. In the pitch black, she was to fight this fight alone.

Chapter 29

For the creatures with no eyes, photonic light made no difference to their vision of the world. They could see through darkness or blinding light. But when Dave bashed the whole lab into darkness, he took out not just the light above the room, but all the power in all the machines. Tied into their fundamental programming was a fail-safe and hard-coded egress. Should the AI mainframe come under attack, the creatures would defend it. In the event of a power outage, Bradley had another fail-safe. There was a battery backup with enough energy to power the mainframe in sleep mode for several days. That usually would be plenty of time to fix the problem.

Freddy and Calla knew that as soon as the power went out, the battery was supposed to work instantly. And in mere nanoseconds, they knew something was wrong.

The battery was actually a raid of several lithium laptop batteries. They were easy to stack in sequence and were cheap. Bradley took them from obsolete old laptops that people threw away.

The problem was that all batteries degrade in cold weather. The batteries in the shed were weak, and very low on power. And as a fail-safe measure, they were not working very well.

The nano-creatures could sense a degradation in the voltage cycle. They ran off to try and fix the problem as their AI parent was working irregularly due to diminished capacity. This was a very different problem from the time when Tessa had pulled the plug. Pulling the plug from the back of the computer now would have cut off power to the electric grid and the laptop batteries. That would have killed the creatures immediately.

As the nano-creatures approached the shed, they were afraid. But they collectively knew they had time and could fix the problem as long nothing else went wrong.

The AI mainframe only needed one battery to run normally. And one battery would give the system five hours of battery life. But six of the seven batteries were completely dead. The last battery was barely holding on to a 5-percent charge now that it had been activated.

This gave the system about 15 minutes of life left.

Freddy and Calla only took a few minutes to get back to the shed. Once there, they quickly got to work. Freddy attempted to remedy their situation.

He was well aware of all steps and contingencies to fix dead batteries. He could materialize tools with his hands. He was precise and didn't make mistakes. Calla stood by him and was proud of what he was trying to do for both of their survival.

Freddy was like a child in the sense that he was not very old. He had internalized human behavior based on what he found on the Internet. They had seen many instances where a man stood over a wire or a bomb or a computer and madly tried to save lives.

The osmosis of mannerisms betrayed Freddy's usual stoic nature. As he fiddled with the fate of his and his sister's life, small globs of sweat appeared on his brow. They were clusters of nanobots forming and falling off him like perspiration from the stressed head of a bomb squad rookie.

Calla tapped her foot on the floor in what

appeared to be a sign of nervousness. This human body tick was not in her programing and should never have manifested itself. As the seconds ticked down on their window of opportunity, even more uncontrollable nervous ticks manifested themselves on her body. She got goose bumps and sweaty palms and turned a whiter shade of pale on her nanoskin.

Freddy kept working, but connectors weren't connecting right, solders weren't soldering right, current wasn't flowing and what should have been a simple fix was turning into a massive problem.

The battery was down to almost 1%. They were running out of time. Freddy was failing. And in the distant background, too far for human ears to pick out, were Tessa's screams, getting louder and more hopeless.

Chapter 30

The cold grip of evil squeezed tighter on Tessa's ankle. The confusion and fear knocked her downward. Tessa, the hero with buns of steel, was on her back. She kicked at Dave, and grabbed whatever she could to throw at him. She even managed to feel around for a metal wastebasket and fling it in Dave's direction. A loud thud followed her release, but adrenaline and madness made Dave unresponsive to pain or bodily harm.

Like a tweeker on angel dust, he received the blows of office equipment to his head and minded not. Blood continued to flow from his forehead as his previous wounds re-opened from the throbbing stress he was feeling. He kept going and reached out with his other hand into the darkness. One half of his brain wanted death to come to his mark; the other half was feeling around in juvenile desire for an errant boob to grope.

Poor Tessa had not anticipated such a quick and deadly response from the mild-mannered stalker who worked beside her. And her cries to her new nano-buddies were going unanswered. Thoughts of defeat flashed in her mind. Visions of imminently losing this battle and ending up like lunchmeat Bradley rose to the forefront of her fears. And somber tinges of regret for the life not lived swelled like the quickening crescendo of a timpani roll.

Dave managed to land a hit. He thrust upward to grab Tessa's left boob. Finally having a handle to hold her, he dug his dirty, unkempt fingernails through her top and into her skin. The pain caused Tessa to scream in agony. She grabbed his hand in return and tried to pull it away, only to be met again with a new hand up against her throat.

Dave, 160 pounds soaking wet, had managed to climb on top of her and use his weight to pin her down. Tessa, 135 pounds of lean muscle, was writhing for her life and kicking to no avail, and he planted himself more firmly on her frame.

Her education and knowledge was failing her. She was running on empty instinct.

Chapter 31

Calla's auditory senses were greater than any human or dog. And in the distance, through walls of plaster and steel, the wails of a brilliant scientist cried for help. She was Calla's friend, or at least the closest thing Calla had ever had to a female friend. And her friend was going to die at the hands of a madman.

Facing impending doom, Calla thought deeply on the unfairness of death.

In her short life she had only met three people. One was dead. Another was fighting for her life. The third certainly deserved to be dead for his crimes. Calla felt new emotions again. Sadness, regret, and a swell of love for her partner, lover and sibling who was trying ever so hard to save them.

The nano-creatures didn't have dreams for the future like people did. They had lists. And Calla often dwelled on her lists. She had checked off just a few boxes. And her regret stemmed from the fact she thought she was done checking boxes. When the battery ran out of juice, all the boxes to be checked in sunshine or on a salty sea would be gone, along with her list and her conscious machine soul.

Freddy was a blur of movement on the floor. He was tinkering as fast as he could. And suddenly, as fast as he began, he stopped. His immediately still shape drew Calla's attention away from her friend's screams and her own deep thoughts.

Freddy looked up at her and made a minor frown. That frown said a thousand words, and she knew what it meant. The end was near. He had tried his best. But the antiquated circuitry coupled with shabby conditions had made a mess of their backup plan. Even a grand technician like Dave couldn't have tinkered his way out of this.

Tessa's screams never ceased during the short try at life. They just grew louder and more desperate.

Freddy was drawn to them too. His meditations on death were entirely different from Calla's. Freddy had been created first. And he was sentient enough to know when Calla was forming from her jumbled mass of nanobots. He had wondered about creation from that very moment, and the bright creation of a life only fascinated him more as he neared the end.

He wasn't sad or scared. Death or deletion was on his list anyway, and he figured this was just a way to skip ahead to the end of the line.

Their shared consciousness grew closer than ever as Calla reached out for Freddy's hand. Once again they chose to act out a trope of human behavior from the movies. He took her other hand and moved closer to her. As the flickering light on the PC grew dimmer, they embraced and were at peace together.

"No!!! " Calla screamed.

She recoiled from Freddy, her skin accelerated its surface swirl, and she screamed again, out loud.

"No, you can't! No, please don't!"

Freddy just gave her that half-grin again. He had made a choice. She knew it the second he made it. Sharing a mind, he didn't have to articulate his intentions except for one last line to calm her fears.

"You can't stop me. I will do it. Now go do what you really want to do. You have little time. Use it well."

Calla couldn't cry and materialize real tears made of water, only fakes ones made of machines. As she stared at him with those metal tears, she silently said everything she needed to say to him.

Then as fast as she'd come to the shed, she sped away at a gazelle's speed to the origin of the screamed words: "Please don't kill me!!!"

Chapter 32

Tessa lay on her back, pinned down by the sweat-soaked and bloodstained frame of an über-killer-nerd.

One of his hands was gripping her throat; the other was clawing into her breast. As she struggled in total darkness, she could not see her enemy before her. He was so close that globs of his blood, sweat and tears hung like suspended ripe pears just a few centimeters from her open, crying mouth.

She recoiled at the smell and swung her head away and back. Doing so, she hit it on a rolling caster from an office chair. The caster had a gripping pin that could be pushed to stop the caster wheel from moving. And that's exactly where her head hit it, thus planting it in place to dig into her scalp as she continued to struggle for freedom.

"Reispt. Bit. Muh fl," Dave mumbled. He no longer clung to normal speech, just grunts and huffs.

His intentions were every bit as primitive. She noticed that a baby carrot size stiffie protrusion wiggled in his pants and pressed into

her thigh. Gross. He grunted some more, and
the whole thing disgusted her so much she
almost barfed in her mouth.

There was still no light. She had to feel
around for something else to use to save her life.
Reaching behind her, she could feel a tangle of
wires under a desk and behind the chair. She
pulled as hard as she could and managed to
come out holding one of them connected to a
small iPhone charger.

Gripping the bottom of the charger like a
stone, she smacked it hard against Dave's
noggin. Again and again and again.

The rapid-fire smacks jolted Dave back
and he let her body parts go. Tessa kicked and
continued to hit him until he rolled over in pain.

"Oooow!" he screamed.

He was able to break free and finally
stand up. She could feel the stuck office chair
next to her. She whipped it around behind her,
hoping it would land on his face.

Her legs went to work as she crawled
and hopped and fell over all sorts of objects
trying to get away. It was so dark she couldn't
get but a few feet before she tripped or knocked

into something new. Each collision with office junk bruised her skin and hurt quite a bit.

She stumbled but then found both feet on solid ground. She stopped and held her breath. She wasn't sure if Dave was near, but the silence scared her. She could not hear him, either.

It was like an auditory staring contest. Or perhaps he had just keeled over and died. All she could hear was her own breath and her heartbeat pounding in her inner ear. Thinking it was best to try some minor move first, she gingerly picked up her right leg and stepped back as quietly as she could.

When her foot landed on the floor, it made no sound that she could hear. She stepped again, then turned around and just walked, hoping to reach a wall, door or window. She felt her way with outstretched hands, and her palms landed on a familiar shape. It was the molding of the door. Then she felt the open hole of the doorway. She went through, grabbed the door and quickly but quietly tried to close it.

She was within inches of sealing the room when an obstruction stopped her. Dave had his foot on the doorjamb, and had been behind her the whole time.

The door caught, and he pushed it back hard on Tessa, hitting her in the head. It knocked her back on her butt. Dave began grabbing for her again, and this time he just reached into the blackness and grabbed a clump of flying hair. Tessa's scalp felt like it was tearing as he jerked her head towards him. He pulled her whole body around and was now pulling her along the floor by her hair.

She grabbed the doorjamb and tried to hold on for a second.

"Stop it, Dave! Stop! Ow! Please don't kill me! Please, please, please stop!" she screamed.

Dave grabbed the door again and slammed it, this time hitting the side of Tessa's head really hard. The bonk almost knocked her out. It dazed her. And in the blackness, her eyes got fuzzy and her mind slowed. Her pleas stopped and her defenses waned. Her body went limp and Dave kept pulling until he pulled her back into the room. He felt around again, and slammed the door shut, closing her exit and her chances.

Chapter 33

Freddy saw Calla go further and further away. His internal clock knew he had but seconds to act. And he did act, at his own peril.

Within the architecture of each microscopic nanobot was a quite beautiful machine. Like the individual cells of the human body, the tiny nanobots had working parts, each with a special job to do. On the outside of each bot was the membrane: the "skin" that could transform into special shapes and colors. Inside there were two more components: the "power plant" of the bot, which was similar to the mitochondria of a cell, and the "hatchlet", which was similar to the lysosome, or waste disposal unit of the cell.

The nanobots ran on power that was culled from electromagnetic waves. The power plant could harvest microwaves, radio waves, or any wave actually, and turn it into electricity. The hatchlet cooled the bot and diverted the excess waste heat. Adding up all the power plants in all the millions of nanobots amounted to a substantial quantity of energy. It was enough to run a lawnmower, treadmill, flat screen TV – even enough to run a computer terminal.

Freddy had made the decision to divert his power right into the power supply of the AI computer. He had enough power in there to run it for almost half an hour. But when each power plant in each nanobot depleted its power, the bot "died" or failed. And like dead fleas, they simply fell off Freddy and drifted onto the floor, dead and useless as iron shavings.

Each bot lost would make Freddy lose mass. Eventually, he would waste away to nothing but a pile of magnetic dust.

To give his power so that Calla could live longer, he would have to die. But he had made his choice, and was fine with it. The sprouts of emotions that he had started to feel over the past day were at their peak. He felt love for her. And he was willing to sacrifice himself so that she could live a little longer and maybe, just maybe, save the life of their friend.

Honorably, he knelt down first, and placed his hand over the battery chords. Small sparks sprang from the connection as tiny veins the size of human hairs flowed from his arm. They ran along the wire into the AC plug. Those veins simply conducted the electricity that was being emitted from the top of Freddy's body.

As the sparks continued, little flakes of spent nanobots fell from him. If an ant had crawled by, and looked up, it would have seemed like black snow was falling all over the shed floor.

To conserve energy, Freddy lost his form, and soon was nothing but a dark black mass of bots slowing fading away. And deep inside that undulating blob was a good-hearted creature hoping this sacrifice would not be in vain.

Chapter 34

Calla stood before the violence and jumped into action.

Dave had hit Tessa so hard that she was dazed out of her mind. Drifting somewhere between sleep and death, she was at the mercy of this madman.

He was dragging her by her hair past the door. He dropped her head between his feet. He intended to stomp on her face. But as he lifted one leg, he lost balance and gingerly put it down again while grabbing a lamp for support.

He lifted his leg again, and while he could not see it, his heel was right above Tessa's face. His smash would certainly break her skull, and likely kill her.

When his knee reached its apex, he held it there before his guesstimate stomp.

Calla's response time was nil. With her love collapsing like a sandy hill on a windy day, she wanted to make sure she could at least save one life.

She extended her arm towards Dave.

And like Mr. Fantastic or Stretch Armstrong, her hand extended past its usual length. It whipped forward at a stunning speed. In the second it took for her extremity to travel, her hand morphed into a pointy awl-like stabbing weapon. It was thin as a pencil at the tip. And when it reached its mark, it wrote a new chapter on making a fucking badass fatality.

The pointy prick stabbed Dave though his shoulder. The speed at which she lashed out gave it enough momentum to penetrate bone and flesh.

Her weapon hand passed through the other side of him. He screamed in agony as his one planted foot buckled at the ankle from the pain.

He fell down, narrowly missing Tessa's head with his knees. He stood over her and looked down for a quick second while Calla did her worst.

The nano-structures shot out of Dave's wound and wrapped around him like a snake. She took several steps towards him while her extended self coiled around his neck, then mouth and then eyes.

He was wrapped like an unlucky bunny

being caught by a snake. The long, wormlike thread kept looping his head further and further until it was completely covered in Calla's grip. The vertebrae in his neck and spine strained.

He had no idea what was happening because it was happening so fast. With all the force she could muster, she pulled her long tentacle back. Her recoil of nano-rope spun Dave's head around like an old top.

His neck muscles snapped, his neck tore and blood spurted around the room like water from a sprinkler head.

It spun 360 degrees, again and again, with such force that only an errant skin flap was left holding it to his body.

A dead and disgusting Dave fell backwards against a desk, where his still-beating heart pumped out the rest of his blood all over the floor.

Tessa was out of it and couldn't really understand what had happened. To her it sounded like a popcorn crunch, followed by a damp thud. She hoped that Dave was neutralized. And then she let her consciousness drift away.

Calla coldly stepped over the bastard, lifted up her hurt friend and took her away from the red stained room.

Chapter 35

There was a soft bed in the corner storeroom. Calla guessed that Tessa's injuries were not too severe. She had saved her friend's life from a madman. And now she just wanted to make her comfortable.

This was an outer room and it had a small window. The moon was shining brightly enough to provide just enough light for human eyes to discern the objects in the room.

Tessa was not fully aware of what was going on. She felt her body being transported; then, as her butt cheeks rested on the soft pillows of a government cot, she saw a blurry shape retreat into the darkness.

Then she looked around the room and noticed a blanket on the floor next to her. She pulled it over her aching body and felt a lot warmer and a whole lot safer, and drifted to sleep to let her noggin heal.

Meanwhile, Calla was racing back to the shed. Once again she jumped over a body, disregarding its presence to focus on getting to the AI as quickly as she could.

The puddles and meat sacks of two maniacs were of no concern to her. All she wanted was to get back to Freddy in time. Then, as she got to the hallway that led to the shed, she saw a reason to run even harder. In the distance, she could see how small Freddy had gotten.

Once inside, she towered over the lump that was left. Freddy was a black blob no more than a foot high. He quivered among the sparks like a gelatin dessert on a bumpy train. And as his body wasted away next to him, he still had enough energy in him to notice the she had come back.

To give her a sign, the top of the little blob made two simple glowing eyes that stared up at Calla. And she stared down at him.

"You are the cutest little blob I've ever seen!" she exclaimed, trying to bring some levity to the grave situation.

He only blinked the glows in return, unable to speak.

She knelt down next to him. She put her hand on top on him. She caressed him and kissed him on the top of his little blob head.

She knew there was not much time left. To prolong her life, she decided to go into sleep mode. Her frame shrank into a tiny little black cube. Even in that state she was fully aware and awake.

She knew that soon Freddy would be dead, and she would be a lifeless blob too. With great sadness, she tried to comfort them both.

She created two little light eyes of her own. And there in the cold, freezing shed, the little blob and the little cube blinked their goodbyes and spoke their love in silent Morse code.

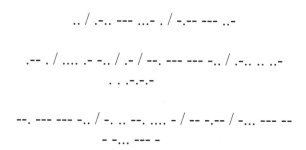

Then all was dark.

Chapter 36

Tessa woke up in the morning. The dim moonshine was now a dim sunshine on her face. It was very quiet. Her head ached, her body ached, and she had only fuzzy recollections of how she got there. Her clearest memory was of crazy Dave attacking her in the dark.

She sat up slowly, and her body ached from her bruises. Finding random cuts and welts slowly reminded her more and more of the ordeal she had suffered. Her thoughts turned to Calla and Freddy. What could have happened to them?

Staggering out of the room she found herself almost barfing at the sight of blood and destruction on the walls of the base. She needed to go back to the scene of the crime.

She was still sleepy, and she needed coffee, but instead she got a double dose of wake-up gore-stink to open up her eyes. The only light in the room came from a window in the hallway. She was able to find a lighter in the utility drawer.

Using the single flame to guide her, she found Bradley's badly mutilated body lying on the floor not far from Dave's headless corpse. Dave's head had managed to land neatly in a cubicle wastebasket.

There was no sign of Calla and Freddy.

"Guys ?!? Where are you?!?"

Getting no response, she went to the shed. That was their special room, after all. Her speed was a snail's pace, but she figured she didn't need to rush. It didn't occur to her what their fate could have been.

"Come on out. Holy shit, it's a slaughterhouse out there! Guys?!? Anyone?!?"

She cut herself off when she finally saw the contents of the red shed. It was cold and dark in there, too. The only light was a low-battery LED warning light on the laptop battery emergency case raid. Next to the case and the quiet PC was a pile of what looked like iron shavings and a small black metal cube.

Smart as she was, it didn't take long for her to put it all together. Her friends were gone. One was a knickknack, and the other was what a person finds in a full dustpan.

Her body sank until she hit the ground.

And then her chin dipped in sadness. Her friends were really gone.

Out of respect for the dead she didn't disturb their remains. She put on a coat from the wall rack, and went outside. There was a pack of cigarettes in one of the coat pockets.

She wasn't a smoker, but she wasn't usually a massacre survivor, either.

The health nut inhaled the sulfurous chemical smoke from an old menthol and froze her butt off outside to catch her breath and get her mind straight.

There were so many possibilities for her next course of action. First she contemplated the most obvious one. It was just to tell the world the truth and let the chips fall where they may. That was out of the question, for the obvious reason that things were so fantastical. She had to think up a better solution than that.

None of her options were easy. By the time the flame met the filter of her cancer stick, she had made up her mind. She dumped the dirty butt onto cold, hard ice, and stomped on it. Then she kicked it away, threw the disgusting pack of cigarettes along with it, and slammed the door.

Tessa needed to get to work.

Chapter 37

Her list was vast and well organized. There was no one there to stop her. The bloody truth of the previous day was going to be erased from history. The clock was going to be turned back. The dead would rise and a brilliant girl from a small town whom everyone underestimated would excel and finally get her piece of the pie. And in her wake, Chip, the small town, the bitches, the scientific community and the world would be left gasping.

Step 1. Turn on the goddamn lights.
It was still dark as shit in the lab. Luckily, the place had backup heat from oil, but it would not last more than a few days.

Since she wasn't an electrician, she had no clue how to fix an ancient fuse box. She went to the only man who did. Dave, über-nerd, was also a closet hoarder. She'd once caught a glimpse of his room and it was all strewn about with books, manuals, porno mags and notes. She figured there had to be an electrical book somewhere.

When she got to his room, it was a complete disaster, and most of the papers were stained in the worst way. But among the filth, she found the schematics to the electrical grid, his notes on why it was terrible and needed to be replaced, and the letters of rejection from the bosses who didn't want to spend the money to fix it.

One page at a time, with a dictionary by her side, she learned his trade. Over hours and a day she found the necessary components. And after 48 hours of tinkering and tottering, she flipped the switch on the generator and it felt good. Let there be light! And there was light all over the Grand Lab. Plenty of light to highlight and bring into view the worst of what the men had brought on themselves.

Step 2. Clean up bloody mess.

Thankfully, they were so far up north that few flies could stand it, which kept the maggot explosion to a minimum. But their bodies were bloated and purple. They stank worse than anything Tessa could imagine.

She had a trash bag in one hand and Dave's head in another when she was unable to make her aim count. When she tried to throw it away, Dave's head missed the opening of the bag and landed on her foot, teeth and mouth first.

"Ahhh, gross!" she yelled.

Fuck that. She decided to skip Step 2 and go right to Step 3.

Step 3. Bring Freddy and Calla back to life (and get them to do Step 2 for you).

This was going to be a hard part. Tessa was smart, but she was not Bradley smart. She could not make heads or tails of his office mess and notes. Days went by as she studied his ways. With Freddy, iron shavings version, in a glass jar, and Calla as a paperweight, she plotted at Bradley's desk to no avail. Then a light bulb went off in her head.

Bradley was keen to be videotaped. His perverted collection must not have been his first foray into documenting his greatness. She went to his tape collection in the shed. There were disks, files, and even some real VHS tapes to look over.

Most of it was crap. Old TV shows. Old porn. Selfies of him jerking off. Finally she found a collection that he'd made as he was ramping up to finally finish his creation.

Bradley had made these video diary-like monologues, in the nude no less, on how he was going to apply this tech. And in between the constant stroking of his ego and the occasional stroking of his knob, he peppered some clues as to how to get started.

It took another week before Tessa had worked out a plan of action. It was by far the hardest intellectual exercise she had ever done. But she felt proud even before she flipped the switch. She knew she had the potential to be as great as Bradley. It was inside her the whole time, she just needed her feet held to the fire, or in this case, to the frozen ice, to push her forward. And without Chip-like distractions, townie-like judgments or parentally founded insecurities, she stepped up to the plate.

"Two peas in the bucket, mutha, mutha fuck it! Here goes everything!" she yelled out loud to herself.

And with that she pressed "Enter" on Bradley's keyboard, setting into motion a surge in several devices, programs and computers. The AI heard her call and the PC went to work.

The small printer that printed the first nanobots hummed like a bird for minutes at a time, while it started to print what would become "seed" nanobots that would rebuild Freddy.

Meanwhile, Calla was on a little platform with copper wires wrapped all around her. The whole thing looked like a kid's science project. But it was Tessa's last hope, and she stepped back, letting science do its work.

Sparks flew, lights popped, and then nothing. Nothing happened.

"No! Dammit!" she cried.

The whole week's work seemed to be for nothing. She looked into the mirror and found herself wanting. She stepped away from the gadgets and ran to her room.

The last bottle of wine was by her nightstand. She crawled into her bed of failure and exhaled. With each swig of vino she told herself that at least she'd tried. She was still smart. But Calla and Freddy were never coming back she thought.

"Maybe there's a little cubicle out there with my name on it. Hopefully with a better class of nerd around it," she said out loud. The wine had taken its toll.

Her eyes felt droopy, and she yawned once more before she clapped the light out on her evening and her chances.

In the cold of the shed, however, there was no sleep, for the life wanted in.

Letting her impatience get the better of her, Tessa had left too early. By the time she went to bed at three in the morning, something was starting to stir in the shavings pile.

The small original "seed" bots created on the inkjet printer were replicating themselves and binding together. The seeds were as big as tiny roly-poly bugs, and they wiggled as much on the floor of the shed. With each sway and micro wiggle, they got a little close to Freddy's shavings pile.

Meanwhile, Calla's cube charged up. And on the smooth surface of her cube top, a microscopic change occurred. A tiny, tiny yellow light appeared. It pulsed a message. A message for Freddy.

-- .. .. / -- . ..--..

Chapter 38

The next morning Tessa awoke with a wicked hangover. She stumbled out of bed into the cafeteria in her panties and nothing else. She made terrible coffee and munched on reconstituted milk and cereal with an ibuprofen chaser.

The almost-nude brainiac had nothing planned for that day. She just wanted to chill, and for once in a long time, not think of anything in particular after a cold run around the base. There were old 80s movies on VHS in the game room. And she had always wanted to learn to play solitaire.

She figured she had at least another three weeks of isolation before someone could come out to get her. There was plenty of powdered milk and bad coffee to last until then. Maybe when she could not stand it anymore, she would clean up the place.

Her silent breakfast was broken when she heard what sounded like music coming from the Grand Lab. It was a small tape player that only had one tape in it. It only played a Sam Cooke's Greatest Hits tape the über-nerds had found in the lab. The tape had Russian writing all over it. It must have belonged to an old serviceman from the other side.

Sam crooned the marvelous words that everyone knows about not knowing about history, biology, science books or the French one took. And how if both knew the love each had for the other, well, what a wonderful world . . .

Tears ran down her face and milk dribbled down her chin. She got up and ran to the lab, not caring about her clothes or morning doofus hair. She got to the door and saw Calla, now manifested as the Morton's salt girl.

"Very nice, Callagirl!" Tessa said.

"Yeah, I thought it was appropriate since she carries her nanobot friends around in a can and spills them behind her all the time."

Tessa stepped closer, beaming with happiness.

"That's a box of salt, honey. But I get the joke. And Freddy?" Tessa asked.

"Well, our little salt baby needs a little more time. But soon, we can stick a fork in him, he'll be all done," Calla replied.

And she revealed a swirling mass of goo and particles in a big cooking bowl. The little blob shook and wiggled as Sam Cooke sang away. One could almost say it looked happy, as happy as a cute Jell-O of molasses could look. It just wanted to grow up and be with its family again.

Chapter 39

Cole idled his plane and turned it off. He let the propeller slowly wind down to a standstill. He had just endured so much turbulence and nerve-racking aviation alarms that he was for the first time in his life considering retiring. The winds of climate change stirred in the future, and the years to come would be filled with worse storms and colder fronts. Risking his life for the low pay of an air taxi didn't seem worth it. He rubbed his Halle Berry photo. The word was she'd gotten divorced, maybe he should move to California and take a shot, he thought. And if he failed at least he could get a second-rate Halle-looking waitress to share his golden years, preferably one twenty years his junior who could share his pension and keep him warm. Such thoughts only upturned the corners of his mouth for a second. He had one more task to get through.

Hopping out of his plane, he was engulfed in ice crystals and fought the frost towards the entrance of the Grand Lab. His mission was to rescue the morons who'd stayed behind. There had been no radio contact or contact of any kind. The world was waiting with bated breath to hear about what had happened to the scientists. And by the world waiting, that meant a couple of lawyers representing the Farrow base against lawsuits, perverted lonely hearts who might no longer have Tessa's rump to jerk off to, Tessa's family and Dave's crazy mother.

The door seemed locked, or at least broken. Cole, being a real man and not a techno geek, put the bottom of his boot up the door's asshole, and it flew open. Bam! The stench emitted from the inside wafted up Cole's nostrils and caused his nose to rumple and tongue to gag.

"Smells like bodissy. Booty, dick and pussy. Hmm, more like jibass. Jizz, balls and ass." There were also hints of cleaning fluid, bleach, blood and human shit in the lab.

"What the mother fuck is going on in here?!? Hello! Hello! I'm here to save your white asses!"

Nothing. Not a peep. But the lights were on. He didn't fear cryptid snowbeasts or other man-eating animals. So he moseyed on in and sighed in annoyance that saving people should be this hard.

He walked down the long hallway, past the dorms, past the cafeteria, until he heard some stirring.

"Hello!"

"I'm here! Cole! Thank god! Holy shit, I'm glad you came. It was awful! So awful!" Tessa yelled as she ran into his arms.

"What happened?"

"Dave and Bradley started fighting. They tried to kill each other. Then Dave ran off and Bradley ran after him. They went out the back and I never saw them again!"

"They just ran out? Why did they fight in the first place?"

"Bradley was protecting me. Dave went mad in here, like he got cabin fever or something. He tried to hurt me. Bradley stopped it. Then they fought. They probably froze to death out there!"

"Hmm. Tessa, I like you and all, and I'm glad you're alright. But you really expect me to believe that story? Dave couldn't force himself on a blowup doll if he tried. You would kick his ass easy. And no way old man Bradley goes out in the show storm after some nut!"

"I'll prove it," Tessa said.

Tessa coaxed Cole into the security room. There was a live-feed recording the events in the Grand Lab the whole time. The system still used a Betamax video machine. When the tape was full, after about 24 hours of use, it just re-wound and started over. This erased it after each time out. There wasn't even a time stamp on it or any sound, just a frame every second.

Tessa played him the footage. The three of them, Tessa, Dave and Bradley, were sitting around talking. Then Bradley got up to leave. Tessa said it was to go potty. Then Dave came on to Tessa. It could be seen that his hand grabbed her boobs and he slapped her. He got up and tried to pin her down against the table. Then Bradley ran in and he and Dave tussled. This sent paper, cards and drinks everywhere. Then Dave ran off to the back door that led to the open mountainside. Then Bradley ran after him. Then the tape stopped.

"That's when I called to them. They never came back. I took out the tape for proof for the police of what Dave tried to do," said Tessa.

Now Cole had both eyebrows raised. But the footage was clear as crystal. It was just like

Tessa said it was. She suggested they go out and look for the bodies. But that suggestion was met with a resounding "no". Cole didn't want to wind up an Ice-e-Cole.

He also wanted to get the hell out of there. He had come during an abnormal break in the weather. Good man that he was, he'd volunteered to try and get the nice lady scientist. And if the other two doofuses happened to be there, he would take them back too.

This tape gave him an out and a reason to cut and run. His eyebrows relaxed.

"Well, shit. Can't argue with video. Better bring that in case the authorities ask any questions," Cole huffed.

As he leaned into the monitor he pressed stop. Right behind him, Tessa tweaked a sly smile and then slipped right back into character.

"So let me grab my stuff, and let's split?" Tessa said.

"Yeah, don't have to ask me twice."

Cole went back and fired up the plane. Tessa was not far behind, but she carried two large suitcases with her.

"Hold on. What's all that shit?!?"

"It's, it's my clothes. Shoes and shit. I'm not leaving it, Cole!"

"Women. Damn. Fine, but you throw it in, girly girl. My back's all fucked."

Tessa lifted the heavy cases into the cabin. Good thing the two weirdoes weren't there, because the cases took up all the other room.

As she buckled herself in, she rubbed her hand on one of the cases. She did it as if she were petting a dog or reassuring a scared child.

She leaned in and whispered, "Almost there."

A bulge undulated from inside the case, then settled back down.

"Ready spaghetti?!?" yelled Cole.

"Yup. Like a big bowl of spaghetti!"

The plane started to advance. It skidded along the snow-covered runway, kicking up white powder behind it. And soon they were airborne.

Free at last.

EPILOGUE

Dorothy Carson ran up the stairs of the Star Island mansion as fast as she could. She was the newest intern. Top of her class at MIT. Her family had been stunned when she took a simple interning gig after college. And at a startup, no less. It hadn't even gone public. Her day-to-day duties varied. But on this day it was getting coffee before briefing the CEO on the upcoming trip to Davos.

Dorothy had a brilliant mind for theoretical physics and mathematics. She'd turned down plum jobs at investment banks and venture capital firms. She believed that only through science could the world's problems be solved. All her life she had wanted to work at a company that could change the world. And upon seeing this particular CEO give a speech at MIT her senior year, she knew that was where she wanted to be.

When she was hired, the CEO picked her personally to work with her, mentor her and give her the respect her beautiful mind deserved. Never would she have to bow to backwards-thinking eggheads who didn't respect her and only had her around to be the token female. Never would she have to be peered at by money-market boors who would objectify her behind her back and sometimes to her face.

So Dorothy didn't mind getting coffee for her new boss now and then. After all, she loved coffee too. And there were great perks at this job. She would get to go on the upcoming Davos trip and hobnob with masters of the universe and TED alumni. And through the conversation, she would be listened to and become known for her ideas.

When she reached the top of the stairs, her boss was waiting for her behind a ridiculously large black walnut desk.

"Thanks a million. And next time, don't go out unless you are getting one for yourself," said Tessa.

Tessa was dressed in a Hugo Boss power suit and held a stack of prep materials in her hand. No running pants in sight. Her slicked back hair, smart makeup and style were looked up to by all the interns. Many of them were female, and they all dreamed of being just like Tessa Hardcastle. At age 37, she was #1 on the Forbes 40 under 40 list of young business leaders. And she was a long, long way from that cubicle at Farrow One.

Tessa slammed the briefing materials down on the desk. The seven folders each had the company logo, name and motto in full color embossed glory:

"Calla + Fred Nano-Robotics"

As far as the world knew, true anthropomorphic nanotechnology was not yet available. It was years away. The company had made enough breakthroughs from the initial deconstruction of Bradley's research without having to exploit Calla's full technology. Tessa was actually responsible for most of the new discoveries. She had a beautiful mind, after all. And once she was in a position to act freely and with confidence, she blossomed and turned out to be a great corporate executive, too.

Dorothy settled in front of Tessa's desk and laid out the materials. She was ready to take notes when a familiar ding of Tessa's computer broke through the mundaneness of the Monday morning. Tessa eyes lit up.

"Oh, let's see where we are today."

She clicked on the link below the subject line "Life's a Beach".

A picture popped up of a handsome

young couple who could be ringers for a young Alain Delon and Sophia Loren. They were holding hands against the sunset on a beach in Puerto Rico. The company yacht floated closely in the background. The caption read, "Saw our first giant clam! Going to the bioluminescent bay tonight! The dinoflagellates in the water light up when excited by touch. Nature's Nanobots! Haha!

Love, C and F"

Tessa's proud eyes squinted downward at her work, so Dorothy wouldn't see her boss's emotions. But her toothy grin betrayed her composure. She was so happy for them.

Free at last. All three of them.

The End

Printed in Poland
by Amazon Fulfillment
Poland Sp. z o.o., Wrocław